FINDING HAPPILY EVER AFTER

ELENA AITKEN

Also by Elena Aitken

Chapter One

WAS SHE BEING PUNISHED? Had she done something wrong?

Natalie Collins took a deep breath and tried to force out at least some of the feelings that started to crowd into her consciousness. No. She wasn't being punished. She was being *rewarded*. That was the worst part.

Ed Walker, who was still the acting fire chief—at least for a few more weeks—was rewarding his rookie firefighter—her—for all of her hard work in the last week.

A reward would be a few days off to sleep in and binge watch Netflix, but with an understaffed fire department in the small mountain town of Glacier Falls, time off was a luxury that wasn't usually extended to a brand-new recruit in the department.

Hero or not.

Ugh. Natalie groaned inwardly at the word. *Hero.*

She was definitely not a hero. Not any more so than any other firefighter. Sure, she'd dragged her partner, Jeremy Davis, out of the burning hotel a week earlier, only a day before responding to a medical callout where she'd delivered an unexpectedly early baby who had no plans to wait until they got to the hospital. But that wasn't a hero.

That was a first responder.

But as uncomfortable as she was with the word, she was even more uncomfortable with the attention she'd been getting from both of those events.

Glacier Falls was a small town, and as such, not a lot of really exciting things usually happened, let alone within a few days. And that was the only reason she was getting attention. Because really, Jeremy had all but rescued his second victim of the fire before getting knocked out by the debris. He was only a few feet away from fresh air, when Natalie dragged him out to safety. He'd done the hard work. Jeremy was absolutely the *real* hero. Which was kind of perfect, considering he was about to be appointed as the new fire chief, too.

And delivering the baby? Anyone would have done it. She just happened to be the one to respond to the call at Ever After Ranch. Hope Langdon was eight months into a high-risk pregnancy when her labor started. It came hard and fast. The only option as the first one on the scene was to deliver the baby, because it was coming with or without Natalie's help. It had been dramatic and stressful and not at all what Natalie had expected when her shift started, but that was how these things went sometimes.

She'd moved to Glacier Falls for a slower pace of life—at least that was the reason she told people. Less than three months later, Natalie was finding her new home and the new friends she was starting to make were anything but boring.

Which was no doubt why the chief had given her the assignment he had. So she'd have a little bit of *boring* in her life for at least a few days.

Little did Ed Walker—or anyone, for that matter—know that being assigned to attend the local high school to teach first-aid classes was not Natalie's idea of boring or a *reward* or an easy assignment or anything short of torture.

High school had definitely not been a positive experience for her, unless you considered the terrible rumors, exclusions, and gossip a positive experience. And she didn't. Worse, growing up in a small community, the drama of Natalie's four years at high school had followed her for many years afterward. A traumatic experience was a massive understatement and the idea of setting foot in the big brick building, walking down the locker-lined hallways that smelled vaguely like a mixture of old gym shoes, pencils, and drug store perfume made Natalie want to turn around and run in the opposite direction or throw up. Or more likely, both.

She was definitely being punished because nothing was worse than returning to a time in her life that she would rather block out entirely.

It didn't matter that Natalie hadn't attended high school in Glacier Falls, but instead hours away in an equally small town on an island off the Pacific Coast, Port Hadlow. A high school was a high school, and as far as she was concerned, Glacier Falls High would be just like her alma mater. Hellish.

Still, she didn't seem to have a choice. Natalie put the pickup truck into park in the guest parking spot and stared at the building in front of her.

She took a deep breath and silently chastised herself.

You aren't a kid anymore. This isn't Port Hadlow. You are a successful woman. They can't hurt you.

She closed her eyes and exhaled slowly before once more opening her eyes and fixing her gaze on the building in front of her.

"You got this." She almost laughed at herself as she opened the door and gathered her supplies from the back of the truck. When she'd been assigned to teach first aid to a group of Outdoor Ed students, she hadn't expected to be so nervous.

Not really. It wasn't until she actually realized she'd be *in* the school and then when she saw the building that all the old feelings rushed back. It had been almost twelve years since her own high school experience, yet somehow those memories had really stuck with her.

Natalie shook off the negativity and refocused her thoughts the way she'd been practicing for over a decade. She wasn't that scared, wounded girl anymore.

By the time she walked up the pathway, with her big duffel bag of supplies and CPR dummy in hand, pulled open the heavy door and set foot in the school, Natalie once again had her signature smile on her face and was ready to go back to school. This time as the teacher.

———

Aiden Adams shuffled the stack of papers in front of him again before turning his attention to the open laptop on his desk and the calendar up on the screen. How was he supposed to fit it all in? Once again he looked to the stack of papers he needed to mark by the next day and then to his calendar. *Maybe there was a small chunk of time after dinner? Before he got a bit of sleep?* With a sigh, he typed *marking* into the empty block on his schedule.

His Netflix binge would have to wait. Just the way it had been waiting since September, when he'd started teaching at Glacier Falls High. He should probably just go ahead and cancel the membership altogether. It didn't look as though he'd actually be using it.

Not that Aiden minded. Not really. He loved being a high school teacher. The challenge of communicating with the kids in a way that got through to them that there was more to life than parties and who was dating who. Not that those things weren't important. But it wasn't that long ago—at least not in his memory—when Aiden was a seventeen-year-old who was obsessed with girls—or at least trying to get them to notice him—parties, and hockey games. He'd grown up on the ice in Ottawa, Ontario, playing goalie for some of the best junior hockey teams. There'd been a time when Aiden thought he'd go all the way to the NHL. School didn't matter. Grades didn't matter. The only thing that mattered was hockey. He had big plans for his life and none of them included school.

Until it all changed on a cold, snowy night coming home from practice on New Year's Eve. His car was hit from the side by a drunk driver who'd been celebrating early. Aiden was lucky to survive at all, not that he would listen to anyone who told him that when he woke up in the hospital with a knee so shattered it would take two surgeries to put it back together. He'd never skate again, at least not competitively. And as far as Aiden was concerned, it would have been better if the woman who'd gotten behind the wheel of her minivan that night had killed him outright.

Without hockey, he had nothing.

No dreams. No future.

It didn't take long for the girls to lose interest in the new, sulky, angry version of him. And not much longer before his old teammates and friends drifted away too.

It took one special teacher, Mr. Stevens, to break through the walls that he'd put up to protect him. One teacher who saw the light in him wasn't completely out. Mr. Stevens pushed and prodded and encouraged him to write about his feelings and experiences until one day, Aiden started talking.

It didn't happen overnight, but gradually Aiden came back to himself. To a new version of himself. All because of a teacher who refused to give up on him.

When it came time to go to college, there was no other choice. He'd be an English teacher, just like Mr. Stevens. And he'd help as many kids as he could.

Still, he shook his head, *it wouldn't hurt to have a little bit of free time to enjoy his new town.*

Aiden blew out a breath and turned his attention to his computer screen and his digital calendar once more. At least he had a spare period now. Time to prepare his lessons and—

"Knock knock."

He tried not to tense at the sound of Megan Cross, the principal of Glacier Falls High. Despite the fact that the woman was at least ten years older than his thirty-one years, *and* the fact that she was his superior and no doubt it was completely against school policy and totally bordered on inappropriate, Megan Cross didn't bother to hide her attraction to him. Mostly Aiden had managed to dodge her advances and not-so-subtle questions about his relationship status.

"I hope I'm not interrupting you."

Aiden turned and put a smile on his face. "Not at all. I was just about to start on some—"

"Oh good." Megan sat, uninvited, on the edge of his desk. "I knew you had a spare period this afternoon, so I was hoping I'd find you right here. And of course I did, because you're always here." She smiled and tucked a piece of her hair behind her ear.

Megan was an attractive woman, but even if she wasn't his boss, Aiden wouldn't be interested. He didn't have time for a relationship *and* a career as a teacher at Glacier Falls High. No way.

"You know," Megan continued, "you have been a huge asset to our faculty, Aiden. I am really glad you decided to join us at Glacier Falls High."

He pushed his chair back and crossed his arms over his chest. This felt like more than flirting. It felt almost as if he were being buttered up for—

"Which is why I need you to take care of something for me."

And there it was.

He nodded knowingly. "I knew there had to be more to it than flattering me unnecessarily."

"Oh no." She looked shocked. "I meant everything I said, Aiden. You are a great teacher and the kids are really responding to you. We've had nothing but positive comments."

"And now you need me to…"

"Take over the Outdoor Ed class."

She spoke so matter-of-factly, Aiden wasn't sure he'd heard her properly. He chuckled. "I'm sorry, I thought you said you wanted me to take over Outdoor Ed."

"I did." Megan crossed her arms and looked at him pointedly.

"But Doug Ivar teaches that class." He didn't need to add that Doug Ivar was the perfect person to teach the class. He wasn't only the head of the phys ed department, he himself was also an avid outdoorsman. In fact, Aiden was looking forward to asking him about some of the trails he should start with when he did have time for some hiking in the spring.

Megan's lips pressed together into a line so thin they all but disappeared. "He did," she said. "But he's out for…well, likely for the rest of the year. He was out back-country skiing on the weekend and got caught up in some sort of *situation*." She used her fingers to make quotes. "He broke an arm and his collarbone, and is in traction with multiple fractures in his leg."

"Holy shit."

"To put it mildly." Megan took a deep breath and pulled her shoulders back. "While he's recovering, the rest of the phys ed department can cover most of his classes, except—"

"Outdoor Ed. Obviously."

"Exactly." She smiled. "You're the only member of the faculty who has an open spot in their schedule."

"But it doesn't make sense." He scrubbed a hand over his face. "That class hikes and backpacks and camps and…I'm a city guy. I just moved here. Hell, I've been so busy with the curriculum, I've barely had time to get outside myself." He didn't bother adding that one of the big reasons he'd taken the job in Glacier Falls was so he could do all of the things he'd just listed. He'd moved for a complete lifestyle change and was looking forward to getting outside and trying some of the activities that the mountains had to offer. Just as soon as he found the time.

"Well, this is your chance then." She stood up as if the matter was settled. "The class meets in the gymnasium."

Apparently the matter *was* settled.

"In period four."

"That's right now." Aiden's head snapped up and followed the principal as she walked across the room to the door.

"It is," she said. "And I suggest you get over there. Doug scheduled in some first-aid training today. A good idea, as far as I'm concerned," she added. "I mean, if you're going to take a pack of kids out into the wilderness alone, the least you can do is prepare them with some basic skills in case they fall out of a tree or off a cliff or something."

His eyes widened and Megan laughed. "Don't worry," she said. "We make their parents sign waivers."

"Perfect."

"It is, isn't it? Just like it will be perfect for you to take over the class. I'll email you the class list and the curriculum Doug had put together." She turned to leave. "The first-aid training is going to take a few classes though, so you'll be able to ease in." She slipped from the room. As soon as Aiden dropped his head to his chest, she popped back in. "Oh, and I meant what I said," Megan said. "You should get down to the gym as quickly as you can. I mean…a bunch of teenagers with CPR dummies…"

"Right." Aiden groaned. "I'm on my way."

Chapter Two

THERE WAS NO TEACHER.

How could there be *no* teacher? It was a high school.

Natalie looked around the gymnasium again. It was a pretty even mixture of girls and guys, which would have surprised her when she was going to school. The girls she'd shared a grade with were a thousand times more likely to go to the mall than anywhere outside. But that was probably representative of life in a mountain town.

Or maybe things were changing.

"Are we going to have to actually *kiss* that?" A girl with jet-black hair and piercing green eyes pointed a long red nail toward the CPR dummy Natalie had placed on the floor in front of her.

"You're not actually going to—"

"I'll practice mouth-to-mouth with you, Lexi."

The girl—Lexi—squealed as a boy wrapped his arm around her waist and spun her around into a deep—and completely inappropriate for school—kiss.

Okay. Maybe not much had changed.

As if Lexi and the boy had sparked a fuse on the group of

kids, they dissolved into laughing, cheering, and a few more couples who'd also decided to *practice mouth-to-mouth* ahead of schedule.

The old but still all-too-familiar sensation of panic started to travel through her body. Her fingers tingled. She couldn't feel her feet at all. It was hard to breathe.

Was she seriously going to have a panic attack because of a bunch of horny teenagers?

No.

She was stronger than that. She'd grown out of that.

Natalie took a deep breath and closed her eyes for a second before exhaling slowly. She was strong and confident, and there was no way she was going to let her past interfere with her present. Nope. She was stronger than that.

She opened her eyes, straightened her shoulders, and prepared to take command. "Okay, class."

Nothing.

The kids were all still laughing and fooling around. They hadn't even heard her.

Fine. She could handle this, too.

Natalie put two fingers in her mouth and let out an ear-shattering whistle that reverberated in the huge gym. Instantly, she got her desired effect and the group stopped. They all turned to stare at her, quiet now.

"Wow."

It was Natalie's turn to be surprised. She jumped at the voice behind her and turned around to find a man so tall, dark, and handsome like every single romance novel she'd ever read in her life that for a moment she thought for sure she was imagining it.

And then he spoke again. "I've never seen anyone who didn't hold the power of their grades in their hands get them quiet so quickly."

No way was he the teacher.

Men that good-looking weren't teachers.

Natalie's heart raced again. This time for a completely different reason. She smiled a little and tried to appear far more confident and casual than she felt. Because, on the inside, her stomach was doing some sort of acrobatic routine that left her breathless without even moving.

She needed to get control of herself.

"Okay, okay." The man, who was most definitely the teacher, spoke to the class. He strode to the middle of the room and crossed his arms over his chest. Like magic, the teenagers, who only a moment earlier had resembled a pack of wild animals, calmed down and started settling themselves onto the mats that had been placed on the wood floor. "I understand we have first-aid lessons today," the man said.

"Where's Mr. Ivar?" a boy called out.

"I'm glad you asked." The teacher smiled confidently. "Some of you may already know that Mr. Ivar had a bit of a ski accident on the weekend."

A round of gasps went around the room.

"Or," the teacher said, "you didn't know." He held up a hand to silence the kids again. "Sorry if it took anyone off guard. And don't worry, Mr. Ivar will be fine. But he won't be back this semester, so—"

A round of groans went through the group.

Mr. Ivar must be a popular teacher. But this guy, whatever his name was, must be pretty popular too. After all, he was definitely the hottest teacher Natalie had ever seen. *Maybe if she'd had a teacher like—* She stopped herself before she could go down that particular line of thinking.

"I'll let him know he'll be missed." The teacher laughed. "But his loss is my gain, I guess, because I'll be filling in for him."

"You? Do you even—"

"Yes, that's right, Zack." He cut the student off smoothly.

"And I'm sure we'll have a lot of fun together. Starting with our first lesson in first aid."

Natalie had completely forgotten why she was there in the school to begin with. *First aid.* Right? That was her.

The teacher, whose name she still didn't know, held out his arm to introduce her. "Class, meet…" He lowered his voice into a half whisper. "I'm sorry, I don't…"

"Natalie Collins. You all can just call me Natalie." She smiled, suddenly feeling self-conscious again as she was put on the spot.

"Well then, Natalie."

It was ridiculous, but she couldn't help but love the sound of her name on his lips.

"Take it away. I'll be right over here if you need anything."

There was definitely one or two things Natalie could think that she might need, but none of those things felt like anything that would be acceptable to say in a high school setting. Or at all to a man she'd just met.

It took her a second before she realized that the group of students, who were now settled nicely, were all watching and waiting for her to say something. Natalie cleared her throat and smiled. First aid was her thing. She'd taught it before and she enjoyed it. Besides, maybe if she pretended that she wasn't having some sort of internal meltdown—first at the whole *being in a high school* thing and now because she was having some sort of intensely physical reaction to the man with eyes so deep and brown they seemed to look straight into her soul—she could get through this.

"Okay," Natalie finally said. "Let's get started. We have a lot to cover today."

Who was she?

Aiden hadn't been in town very long, but long enough to know…well, at least some people. And he definitely didn't know the perky blonde with the long ponytail that bounced behind her as she walked around the gymnasium full of kids and supervised the splints they were creating on their partners.

From the moment he heard her whistle and take command of the students so easily, he'd been drawn to her. And if it hadn't been that, it would be the way she so confidently led the group in the first-aid techniques. She handled their smart-ass comments with ease, and seemed to navigate it all easier than most people. Teenage kids were hard. *Very hard.* And a group of them…damn. It wasn't for the faint of heart.

If she wasn't sure of herself, she was a pretty damn good actress. Either way, Natalie Collins had all of Aiden's attention.

The class went by quickly and before he knew it, the bell rang to dismiss the class and signal the end of the day. To Aiden's surprise, most of the kids didn't rush for the door the moment the bell sounded.

"Can we stay, Mr. Adams?"

"Just to practice a little bit more?"

"I almost have the perfect sling, Mr. Adams. Look."

He didn't even bother hiding his surprise. "I wish I would see some of this enthusiasm when we're talking about Hamlet," he joked. "I don't think any of you volunteered to stay late to discuss if Hamlet had truly gone mad or not."

He didn't wait for a response, but crossed the floor to Natalie, who was packing up her bag with all her supplies. "Class was great today, really. Thank you so much."

She turned and offered him a sweet smile. "You don't think I bored them too much?"

"Are you kidding?" He waved his arm. "Look at this. They just asked if they could stay a little later and *practice* their bandaging." Aiden shook his head. "You must be a miracle worker. I don't know if you know much about high school students, but they *never* want to stay late." He thought he might have seen her smile dim as he spoke, but then it was back. A full, warm, bright smile.

Between that smile and her sparkling blue eyes, Aiden was having trouble looking away from Natalie.

"Well, that's good," she said. "I actually get really passionate about first aid." She laughed. "I know that's a silly thing to say, but…you know what, I still don't know your name, Mr. Adams."

Aiden was taken aback. Had he not introduced himself? It seemed like a terrible oversight, particularly because Natalie was…well…stunning and completely engaging. Her energy drew him in. "I'm so sorry," he said. "I sometimes forget that I'm not just Mr. Adams." He extended his hand. "Aiden," he said. "Aiden Adams. I teach English, and well…now Outdoor Ed."

"Nice to meet you Aiden Adams, English and now Outdoor Ed teacher."

The moment she took his offered hand, there were sparks between them.

Natalie made a small squeaking sound and jumped back. "Oh my goodness. I'm sorry. These bandages sometimes get staticky and it's so dry in here…"

Aiden laughed. "I don't know, some would say there's electricity between us."

Did he seriously just say that? "Some would say that?" Who would say that? Not him. He fought the urge to groan and duck his head.

Fortunately, she didn't laugh at him. Instead, she continued talking about first aid, which, ironically, was a safe subject. "I actually think it's really great that your school is doing this," Natalie said. "Everyone should know basic first aid, and then you know… if any of your students were interested, there are more advanced first-aid classes that would be really great for them. It could be a really great complement to your course. There's a specialty program for wilderness first aid and although I've never taught it myself, I'd be happy to do some looking into it if you're interested."

"Oh, I'm interested."

Again, he could smack himself. For a guy who'd never, not one time in his past, lost his composure with a woman, he was not doing a good job playing it cool with Natalie.

"I mean," he recovered, "I'm sure some of the kids would be interested in that. I still need to take a look at the curriculum that Mr. Ivar laid out and see what I'm in for this semester. But I'm sure whatever it is, it's going to be challenging for all of us."

Natalie tucked away a stack of brochures in her bag. "I'm sure you'll do great."

"You know, if you want to join us on some of our treks, it might be a good idea to have someone along who knows—"

"OMG! Are you that firefighter lady who delivered the baby!" Simone, a student with a stack of bandages in her hand, interrupted them. "I mean, I don't know why I didn't think of it earlier, but my mom said a female firefighter like totally caught Hope's baby. Was it you?"

Natalie took the bandages from the girl and put them in the bag with the others. She blushed with the attention, her skin pinking around her ears. "It was."

"I knew it."

"And, I am the only female in the department, so…" She shrugged.

"You are?" Simone stared at her. "Really? Holy sh—"

"Careful," Aiden warned the girl. "You're still on school property."

"I was going to say, holy sh-mokes."

Aiden nodded and rolled his eyes, and Natalie laughed.

"Holy sh-mokes indeed. It was pretty incredible, but I'm just glad I could be there."

Natalie patiently answered Simone's questions for a few more minutes before finally the girl left, along with the rest of her classmates.

"You delivered a baby?" he asked as soon as they were alone. "That's amazing."

She shrugged. "You didn't hear? I didn't think there was anyone in town who hadn't heard about it and really, it wasn't a big deal. It was just...first aid." Natalie laughed and finished zipping up her bag before hoisting it up over her shoulder. "More reasons for everyone to learn," she added as she bent to pick up her CPR dummy. "I guess we'll get to this in our next class. Next week, same time?"

Aiden nodded, even though he wasn't really sure of the Outdoor Ed schedule at all, but that sounded right. "Let me help you with that." He took the dummy from her before waiting for a response. To his pleasure, she didn't resist. Even if it was just a few more minutes, Aiden was happy to spend more time with her.

"Thanks again," he said once she'd loaded up her truck with her supplies. "It was really nice meeting you and..."

He hesitated. *Why?* He wanted to ask her out, because... well, because of everything he'd been feeling for the last few hours since they'd met. But despite his ridiculous attraction to the woman, there was no way he could ask her out. He could barely find time to watch a television show, let alone go on a date.

But a date with Natalie would be a whole lot more fun than any television show he could think of, so...

"Think about the outdoor survival classes, okay?" She spoke before he could man up enough to ask her out. "I'll do some looking into it for you and—"

"Join us on our hike next week."

Aiden blurted it out before he'd even realized what he was saying. Was there even a hike scheduled? He had no clue.

"What? A hike?"

"Yes." He hoped he appeared more confident than he felt. Even if there wasn't a hike on the schedule, he'd put one on it. "First aid is…Thursday?" He hoped he'd guessed right. When she nodded, he smiled. "Right. And the hike is during Tuesday's class."

"It is? But it's February. There's snow…"

"It's more of a snowshoe. Maybe. But it might just be a hike." He was fully aware of the hole he was digging, but he couldn't seem to stop himself. And if Natalie noticed that he was totally full of bullshit, she didn't say anything.

"I'll have to look at my shift schedule." She closed the tailgate. "Can I let you know?"

"Of course." Aiden stepped back and offered her a small wave. "Thanks again for today."

He watched as she climbed up into the truck with the Glacier Falls Fire Department logo emblazoned on the side. When she flashed him one more of her gorgeous smiles and offered him a little wave as she drove away, it was only then that Aiden realized that even if he didn't currently have time in his life for a relationship, he would do anything to find it.

Sleep was overrated anyway.

Chapter Three

IF SOMEONE HAD TOLD Stephanie Starz, one of the world's hottest movie stars, a year ago that she'd be in a small-town hospital in the middle of the mountains, staring at a newborn baby, she would have thought them completely insane.

But Steph's life had changed so dramatically in less than a year that very little surprised her anymore. Including the love she had felt instantly and intensely for the tiny baby boy in front of her.

Her nephew.

He had cords and wires and different types of tubes monitoring his levels and providing oxygen, and she couldn't hold him. Yet. But she'd settle for stroking his thin, delicate skin with one finger through the portal hole in the incubator while the machines monitored all his vitals.

Little Cole was born less than a week earlier in what had turned out to be a very dramatic series of events when Stephanie's half-sister Hope had gone into early labor. There hadn't been time to get her to the hospital, and because they were out of town on the Ever After Ranch where Hope, her twin sister Faith, and their husbands ran a wildly successful wedding business, when the firefighters, who were first on the scene, arrived, there'd been no choice but to deliver the baby.

Thankfully, besides being about a month premature, born to a mother with her own health issues, Cole's prognosis was good.

"He just needs to build up those lungs," Hope said from her wheelchair. "But he's a fighter. He'll be okay."

Steph didn't miss the emotion in her sister's voice. She turned away from the baby and gave her sister her full attention. "He *is* a fighter," she said. "Just like his mother." Steph squeezed her sister's hands in hers, and Hope dropped her chin to her chest.

But only for a moment before lifting it again and nodding.

"That he is." She forced a smile, but Steph could see how tired she looked. Her eyes were red from a combination of crying and lack of sleep, and her sister's entire body looked frail and so much smaller than it had only a week ago.

"When do you start—"

"I won't start any treatments until Cole is home and out of the woods."

Hope's vehement response took Steph off guard. That hadn't been the plan. Hope was diagnosed with uterine cancer prior to getting pregnant with Cole. The pregnancy had been a decision Hope and her husband Levi had made along with the blessing of Hope's doctor as long as the cancer stayed under *control.* Which it had, with the help of some low-dose hormones and then the pregnancy itself. But the plan had always been for Hope to start treatment immediately upon the birth of the baby. She would have surgery, followed by some drug treatment just to be sure the cancer was gone. She had a very good prognosis for a long and healthy life. *If* she went ahead with the treatment as soon as possible.

"But you need to—"

"Make sure my baby is okay." Hope pressed her lips

together in a hard line. "That is my only job right now. End of story."

It wasn't hard to see that Hope wasn't leaving much room for discussion or debate on the issue, but still, Steph couldn't help herself. "But, Hope, if you aren't—"

A hand on her shoulder stopped her. Steph turned to see Levi, the proud new father. The look in his eyes told Steph all she needed to know about pushing the issue. She closed her mouth. For now.

"How are you doing today, Daddy?" Steph threw her arms around him and squeezed. "Things have been pretty crazy. Have you gotten any sleep since I last saw you?"

The night the baby had been born, Stephanie was in the city with her friend Bella Burton, who also happened to be her co-star in the upcoming film *Bombshell* that was set to be a mega hit. They'd been performing in a showcase of songs for the new movie as a publicity event. Steph had used her helicopter to fly out Bella's now-fiancée Jeremy, who'd been injured in an accident earlier in the day at a fire he was fighting. So when the news came in about the baby, Steph hadn't hesitated to jump on the helicopter and fly back to Glacier Falls to be with her family.

There were some definite perks to being insanely wealthy.

But all the money in the world couldn't have made Cole breathe on his own, and when the baby had been moved to the hospital, Steph, along with everyone, hadn't been able to visit right away. She'd stayed for a day and then had to head back to the city to take care of some business. But now, she was back and ready to shower her new nephew with all the love and gifts she could before once more returning to work.

"I've definitely got a few more hours than Mama." Levi kissed his wife on the cheek lovingly and smoothed back her hair. He looked at Hope with love and worry. Definitely there was concern in his face as he watched her. "Did you get a nap in, Hope?"

She shook her head and kept her gaze focused on the baby. "Can you just move me a bit…"

Automatically, Levi moved the wheelchair closer to the bassinet, and Hope reached inside. She stroked the tiny hand with one finger and shifted so baby Cole had his tiny fingers wrapped around hers.

Something in Steph's chest clenched at the picture in front of her. When she looked to Hope, she saw one single tear slip down her cheek, but her face was set in a mask of resolution. Steph had no doubt that her sister would *will* the baby healthy, if that's what it took.

"How long are you here for, Steph?" Levi asked. "And where are you staying?" he added as an afterthought. Steph had been staying at the Ever After Ranch with all of them, but with the new baby now, things were about to get crowded and a lot more hectic.

"I'm staying at ElkView Ridge," she said. "In Damon and Katie's guest house."

"That sounds like a great solution. I heard they moved into the main house when Damon's dad moved into the nursing home, which means …"

"The guest house is empty," Steph finished. "I would have grabbed a room at the Big Rock Inn. But the fire kind of took care of that plan."

"Wow." Levi shook his head. "Did it ever. Does anyone know what caused the fire yet?"

Steph shook her head. "Jeremy said the inspector is thinking it was old wiring, but there's nothing official yet."

"Well, we're just all glad everyone was okay. Especially Jeremy. What a hero he was."

Steph nodded. "And Natalie. And then…"

"I owe her everything." Hope's voice was low, and she never looked away from Cole. "If she hadn't…"

"It's okay, babe." Levi put his hand on her shoulder and squeezed. "But she was there, and Cole is going to be fine. We're *all* going to be just fine."

Steph's heart squeezed for the new family. They had so much to go through in such a short time—with Hope's illness and Cole's rocky start in the world. It wasn't what either of them had imagined when they'd fallen in love as teenagers. But they were strong. They'd be okay. And Steph would do absolutely everything in her power to make sure of it.

Steph only had a few more days before she'd have to head back to the city and prepare to go to Los Angeles to start shooting *Bombshell*. As excited as she was to get back to filming, which was something she absolutely loved, she was also sad to leave Glacier Falls, the town she'd learned to call home in the last few months since stumbling upon it when she was planning her own wedding. The fact that she'd never actually married Dax Combs was only a minor detail that she hardly even thought about anymore, especially because although she'd lost that relationship, she'd gained the relationship of the half-sisters she didn't even know she had, and the massive extended family that she'd inherited along with Hope and Faith.

But Steph still had a few days before she had to get back to work, which was perfect because as well as her movie projects, she'd also recently branched out into a brand-new venture.

Carefully, on the snow-packed roads, Steph navigated her four-wheel drive SUV down the windy road off the highway and pulled up to her latest project and the one that, even though she'd barely started on it, filled her heart with happiness.

Lynx Creek.

The collection of cabins nestled into the trees in the bend of the river, just outside of town limits, used to be an old fishing camp. All but one of the cabins, and the main lodge itself, were in desperate need of repair. She'd hoped that she'd be able to live out at Lynx Creek while the renovations were underway, but that plan, ambitious on its own, was thrown for loop when baby Cole came early. The cabins were far from ready. And with the snow expected to stay at least a few more weeks, she was better off staying with Damon and Katie Banks whenever she was in town for the next few months. And depending on her shooting schedule and how smoothly it all went, she couldn't be sure how much that would be.

Although…maybe she *could* start staying up at the cabins.

A sense of calm filled her, and she hadn't even stepped out of the car yet. It was one of the main reasons she'd purchased the old fishing camp—the extreme peace and soul-filling happiness the mountains gave her. Now, she owned a little piece of that happiness that she could call her own. And, when the renovations were complete, she'd be able to share with others, too.

Steph got out of her car, and inhaled the fresh, crisp air, letting it fill her lungs.

Her vision was to create a retreat type of space so others who felt the need to calm themselves and recenter their lives, the way she had, would have a beautiful place to do it.

The sound of a saw ripping through wood shattered the quiet and jarred her from her thoughts of what Lynx Creek would one day be.

Travis?

She hadn't seen the contractor's truck when she'd pulled up, but that didn't mean he hadn't driven in closer to one of the other cabins. Steph's body reacted instantly and dramatically to the thought of Travis Bishop, the contractor and general handyman she'd hired to do the work for her at Lynx Creek. She wasn't usually the type of woman to swoon around a man, or to react strongly at all, really. Usually it was the other way around. With her petite curves and fiery red hair, Stephanie had no trouble attracting men. Stephanie usually reserved her attraction until she got to know a guy and what he was all about. That's what she thought was attractive. The core of a guy, not just his looks. Especially working in Hollywood. She was surrounded by attractive men, and most of them knew how good-looking they were. But a surprisingly small amount of them had much more than their looks as top qualities. She'd been burned too many times by men who pretended to be something they weren't.

Even when she thought she'd landed a good one—Dax Combs—she'd been wrong. With her star so much higher than his, Dax was only out for one thing when it came to marrying her: increased stardom. He wasn't a bad guy. Not really. But she wasn't interested in being with anyone who, when they looked at her, only saw a way to benefit.

No thanks.

Not anymore and not again.

Next time she opened her heart, it would be for real love. Because someone genuinely cared about who she *was*. Not what she could do for them.

Not that she was thinking that Travis Bishop was going to be that guy. Not at all. But she wasn't above admitting that not every relationship had to be about love. Some of them could be based on pure, physical attraction. Which was exactly what she felt for—

"Hey. I didn't hear you pull up."

Steph was jarred from her daydream about the very subject of that daydream. She hadn't even noticed him walk up.

It wasn't a particularly warm day—after all, it was mid-February—but still, Travis wore only a plaid flannel shirt—that he somehow managed to make look ridiculously sexy—and his trademarked worn jeans, this time with a tool belt slung around his hips. His cowboy hat was perched on his head, but instead of the leather boots Steph remembered from their last meeting, he wore some kind of work boot on his feet instead. Safety first.

She took her time looking at him while she caught her breath and composed herself. A task that was made all the more difficult because she was staring directly at him.

Damn. It was impossible not to get worked up around the man. He just did something to her. It was like nothing she'd ever experienced before.

"I didn't know you were here."

His smile was slow and sexy as it slipped into place. "I told you I'd be here."

"Right, but…I didn't see…"

Shit. When she'd texted him to let him know she was in town for a few days, he *had* said he was going to be on-site.

"I parked by the bankside cottage." Travis gestured with the board he was holding. "It was just easier with a truck full of supplies. I guess you didn't see me."

There was no way that the man couldn't see how flustered he made her, not unless he was completely unaware of women altogether, and Steph got the distinct impression that was not the case with Travis Bishop. Not that she'd been able to learn much about the man from her gentle probing of her friends. All they said was he was a very hard worker who devoted himself to whatever project he was on, and he was the best at what he did. Steph couldn't help but wonder what else he might be the best at.

"And how are things going then?" She shifted straight into business mode. Whatever it was that Travis was good at, she needed him to be good at renovating her camp. That was the most important. What was *not* important was letting her feelings or her physical attraction for the man, or whatever it was, get in the way of getting that job done. Besides, it would be easier to keep that side of her under control, if she kept it professional.

She took a step toward the trail, but her boot caught in the snow and she pitched forward.

Moments before going face first into the snowbank, Travis's strong, and noticeably muscular, arms wrapped around her waist and caught her. She sucked in a sharp breath and willed her racing heart to settle down. A racing that had absolutely nothing to do with the fall and everything to do with the catch.

Without releasing her, Travis carefully righted her, so Steph once again stood on solid footing. "It's a good thing I was here."

She looked up into his blue eyes. "It is."

Was it her imagination, or had he held her gaze a little longer than necessary?

She stepped away and pulled her shoulders back in a renewed effort to regain some composure.

So much for professional.

Chapter Four

IT HAD BEEN two days since Natalie's first-aid class at the high school and, to her surprise, she was actually looking forward to going back to teach it again. And no, she told herself again, it had nothing to do with the sexy Outdoor Ed teacher with the dark eyes and smooth voice. And even if it did, she had no business dating a man like that. Not that she knew anything about him. At all.

And he *had* asked her to join him on a hike.

Them, she reminded herself. He'd invited her to join the class. Not him. It wasn't a date.

Which was probably a good thing. Natalie hadn't been on a date since...well, had she *ever* been on a date?

Not unless you counted her freshman year with Brandon Ryan when he took her to the Fall In school dance. And she didn't. Because that had been the night that ruined her life—at least, her high school life. She'd been so excited for that dance. So sure it would change her life. She'd been right. Her life had changed. But not for the better.

Still. Things were different now. She was older and she was over it.

Mostly.

But she'd never forget the whispers, the rumors, the lies, and, worst of all, the way all of her friends believed Brandon's word over hers and cast her out.

Yeah, high school was not fun. Natalie groaned, just thinking about those days.

"Oh no!" Katie Banks, whom she'd only met once or twice, stopped next to her in front of the dairy case where she'd been lost in her daydreams. "Don't tell me they're out of coconut yogurt again," Katie said with a groan of her own. "If I bring lemon home again, Damon will...well, he'll just have to do the shopping himself." She laughed and it was contagious. "Hi. It's Natalie, right?"

Natalie grinned and nodded. She'd liked the outspoken brunette the few times she'd met her at the Hub, Katie's new adventure store that rented and sold all kinds of gear for the myriad outdoor activities that Glacier Falls offered. "And you're in luck." She reached into the dairy case. "They have coconut." She handed the other woman the yogurt.

"Oh, thank goodness." Katie put it in her cart. "But I don't understand. If they have coconut, why the groaning? Are you okay?" Instantly, her smiled dimmed and she looked at Natalie with genuine concern. "I mean, you don't have to tell me, but I can't help but ask when I see a friend looking so..." She waved her hand in the air. "Well, so conflicted."

"Friend?" Natalie couldn't help herself. She instantly felt like a fool for asking, but...it had been a long time since she'd made a new friend. Co-workers didn't count. But a real friend...

"I hope I'm not being too forward," Katie said. "But Glacier Falls is kind of a small town, and I know you're new and then after the way you helped out Hope and the baby, well, you just seem like my kind of people."

"No," Natalie said quickly. "No. You're not being too forward at all. And the baby, well… I was just—"

"Do not tell me that you were just doing your job." Katie held up a hand, stopping her from saying just that. "Because yes, you were doing your job, but from what I understand, you did it with such compassion and care that you really helped to calm Hope down. I've known those girls long enough to know that that is no small feat. So that makes you a hero on a completely different kind of level." She laughed and Natalie blushed. "And besides, the Turner twins are some of my best friends, and so by default that makes you my friend, too."

Natalie couldn't help but laugh right along with her. If Katie was going to force friendship upon her, she'd be more than happy to accept it.

"So anyway…" Katie changed the subject quickly. "You okay? You looked a bit…concerned when I walked up."

A million things that she *could* say raced through Natalie's head, but ultimately, she went with the truth. Well, part of the truth. After all, it wasn't usually considered good form to lie to a new friend. "It's just that I was asked to go on a hike with a group of students at Glacier Falls High and quite honestly, I don't—"

"Say no more." Katie grabbed her hand and started to pull her away from her cart. "Let's get you to the shop and—oh, wait." She turned and shrugged. "Maybe we should finish up with groceries first and *then* let's meet at my shop. Let's say an hour?"

"Sounds good." And it did. Natalie felt drawn to Katie in a way she couldn't remember ever feeling with another female since early on in high school. Before the girls she'd thought were her best friends in the whole world all turned out to be back-stabbing gossips set to destroy her entire life.

But Katie wasn't like that. She watched her new *friend* move away down the aisle with the promise of seeing her shortly.

Maybe Glacier Falls really would be the new start she'd been looking for.

Just over an hour later, as promised, Katie was waiting for Natalie in the Hub. As soon as she'd told her about the hike or snowshoe, or whatever it was—which she hadn't even formally been invited to, or actually accepted—Katie went to work, pulling appropriate winter boots off the shelves and piling them up in front of where Natalie sat, trying on pair after pair.

"These seem okay." She wiggled her toes in the boots. "I mean, they fit."

"But are they warm enough?" Katie turned from where she stood at the shelf, another pair of much bigger boots in her hands. "You said you were going *hiking*? Not snowshoeing?"

Natalie shrugged. "That's what he said. A hike. *Or* a snow-shoe. He wasn't actually very clear on what it was."

"Hmm…" Katie put the big boots down and moved to a different part of the store, hollering over her shoulder as she went. "Who did you say the teacher was? It's not Doug Ivar, is it? Because I usually know about his trips."

"No." Nat got up and crossed the store. There were a few other customers shopping and because she wasn't really sure who anybody in town was, she didn't want to say anything that could be overheard or taken the wrong way. "Not Doug," she said when she got closer. "He was in an—"

"Oh my goodness." Katie's hand flew to her mouth. "You're right. Doug was in that terrible accident in the back country. I can't believe I forgot. Really, I'm not usually so scattered."

Natalie didn't think Katie seemed scattered at all, just maybe *enthusiastic*, but she didn't bother saying so.

"What a terrible thing," Katie continued. "So that makes sense then that he's not teaching it. Who took over?"

Natalie worked to keep her voice neutral and not give away the fact that every time she thought about the man she'd only met the one time, her stomach did a crazy summersault thing that scared her more than a little. "I think his name is Aiden Adams."

"You think?" Katie raised an eyebrow.

There was no way Katie could tell that she was interested in Aiden Adams.

Was she? Interested?

No.

Yes.

Maybe.

She didn't know. But either way, was Katie picking up on something?

"I mean, I…"

"You should probably know the guy's name if you plan on going on a hike with him, right? I mean…"

"Oh yes." Natalie blew out a breath. "I agree." She nodded, as if she'd just figured it out. "It's Aiden. Aiden Adams."

"The new Outdoor Ed teacher?"

Both women turned. The man who spoke was ridiculously tall and gorgeous, with dark hair and a smile aimed straight at Katie. Damon Banks. Katie's husband.

"Natalie, right?" He extended a hand to her, which she took with a smile and a nod.

Was everyone in this town so friendly?

Yes. From her limited experience, almost everyone she'd encountered, with the exception of a very few from the callouts she'd responded to, were all very friendly.

"Sorry," Damon continued. "I didn't mean to interrupt, but are you talking about the new Outdoor Ed teacher?"

"We are," Katie answered for them. "Natalie is teaching a first-aid class for them and she's going on a hike with them next week."

Damon's broad grin split his face. "It's a winter hike." It wasn't a question. "Nothing too major, just an out and back on Rainbow Ridge, where the snow shouldn't be too deep."

Katie crossed her arms and narrowed her eyes. "How do you know?"

"Because he was just helping me figure out where I should take the class on a hike in the middle of February."

Natalie's stomach flipped at the sound of his voice. Her entire body warmed and she knew without having to look in a mirror that she likely had an instant and ridiculous smile on her face.

Aiden.

———

Aiden hadn't been imagining it. It *was* her. When he'd looked across the store and seen the tall blonde who occupied almost all of his waking thoughts for the last few days to see that she was shopping for *hiking boots,* that could only mean one thing.

Well, it could mean a lot of things, but Aiden hoped like hell it meant she was going to go on the hike with him and his class.

The hike he was spending his Saturday trying to organize. A Saturday he should have spent grading papers and organizing his schedule for the next few weeks. But none of those things seemed nearly as important as going on a hike with Natalie—and his class. Obviously, his class. That was the most important thing. Not impressing Natalie.

But that was coming a close second.

A *very* close second.

"Hi." He raised his hand in a slight wave. Without taking

his eyes off her, he smiled. And it wasn't his imagination that she turned a very slight, but very sexy shade of pink. A detail he liked. A lot. "Damon was helping me out with the hike I'd planned."

Damon raised his eyebrows and shook his head.

"Okay," Aiden came clean, "I hadn't planned it yet. Not really. But, in my defense, I just found out about taking over the Outdoor Ed class."

"Right." Damon, whom he'd just met, didn't bother trying to hide his disbelief.

Aiden shot him a look. Wasn't there some kind of bro code or something? He should have his back.

"Well, it sounds like if you're going up on Rainbow Ridge, it will be a great hike and you won't even need snowshoes. Hi, I'm Katie." The woman thrust her hand out at him. "I used to help out Doug Ivar with equipment for his class, so if you need anything at all, let us know. We'll help you out."

"Thank you, that will be a huge help." It really would, because he was in completely over his head. "I'm going to take you up on that."

"Please do." Katie grabbed Damon's arm and started to pull him away. "I think Natalie was going to try on a few pairs of boots," she said. "Maybe you could give her your opinion, Aiden. Damon and I have to sort the snowshoes, so we'll be right over—"

"We do? I didn't think—"

"We do." She shot her husband a look, and Aiden had to look away so he didn't laugh. They were very obvious. "Let us know if you two need any help, okay?"

Katie managed to successfully drag Damon to the other side of the store, and when they were alone, Aiden turned to Natalie, who lifted her shoulders in a shrug.

"That wasn't very subtle, was it?"

"Not at all." He chuckled. "But I'm not going to lie and say

I don't appreciate her effort." There it was, the slight pinking of her skin again. "So," he decided to change the subject, "you're coming on the hike with us on Tuesday?"

She shrugged again. "Why not? I mean, especially since you went to all this effort to plan it." She grinned and added, "After you invited me."

He held up his hands. "Okay, you got me. There was no hike planned. I only invited you because I really wanted to spend more time with you."

"No way."

Her sarcasm was sexy as hell.

"I know," he said, playing along. "It's hard to believe that I'd make something like that up, but I just…" For a second, he debated playing it cool again, but really? What was the point? "I wanted to spend more time with you."

She dipped her head, but he didn't miss the smile on her lips. Was she shy? She hadn't struck him as the shy type when she'd been instructing the class. Quite the opposite. She'd been in control and in command. It was sexy. *Very* sexy to see a woman with that kind of confidence.

This was different.

But also, endearing.

"Did I embarrass you?"

"No." She looked up, and straight into his eyes. "I'm wondering why you didn't just ask."

"Ask what?"

"Ask me out."

And there was that bold confidence again.

Damn. This woman was such a contrast. He couldn't figure her out.

And he liked it.

"Fair enough." Aiden crossed his arms over his chest. "Let me remedy that. Let me buy you a coffee."

She tilted her head so her long ponytail fell over her shoulder. "Is that you asking me out?"

It was lame. Aiden knew it, and he knew he could do better. *A lot* better. But there was no time like the present, and he didn't want to risk missing his opportunity completely. "Okay, let's not call it a date," he said. "Let's call it a *coffee*. We'll start there." He flashed her a smile he hoped would convince her to say yes. Because he hoped like hell she'd say yes.

It had been a long time since he'd been drawn to a woman the way he was with Natalie. A *very* long time. If ever.

She shook her head slightly and opened her mouth to turn him down, no doubt.

No way. "Did I say coffee?" He interrupted her before she could say what he was sure would be a rejection. "I meant, coffee *and* a honey bun from Sweetie Pies. Maybe you can say no to me. Or even a coffee. But no one can say no to a honey bun."

She burst out laughing and nodded. "Okay."

"Okay?" Aiden didn't bother trying to hide his joy. No point in playing games. "It's a date?"

"No." She held up a finger. "It's coffee *and* a honey bun." Her smile gave her away. "And, for the record, I would have said yes just to the coffee."

Chapter Five

SHE'D SAID YES.

Natalie still couldn't believe she'd said yes to a date—or a *coffee*—with Aiden.

But why not?

She wasn't a teenager anymore. She was almost twenty-eight, for goodness' sake. Long past time to go on an actual date, never mind what might come from that date, or subsequent dates.

Natalie's skin flushed and something low in her belly tightened at the thought.

No.

She could not let herself think about that.

About *sex*.

Or the fact that she'd never had it.

After all, it was hard to have sex when you hadn't even hardly kissed a man.

But no, she couldn't let herself get carried away. After all, it was just a coffee. A coffee *and* a honey bun, she corrected herself as Aiden turned from the counter of Sweetie Pies, where he was placing their order. He smiled at her.

Damn.

How was it that a man could make her feel so twisted up and turned around with a simple smile? It was ridiculous and amazing. But still, she was getting ahead of things.

Natalie forced herself to take a deep breath and focus on the moment and only the moment as Aiden approached the table with a full tray.

"I didn't know how you took your coffee, so I brought a little of everything." He set the coffees down, followed by the plate of honey buns that Sweetie Pies was famous for, and then started placing tiny cups in front of her. "This one is cream. This one is almond milk. This one is skim and—"

She stopped him before he placed the other three cups down. "I almost hate to say this, but..."

"You drink it black, don't you?" His face fell, but only for a second before he laughed. "I should have known."

"It's just easier to drink it black," she said as he started putting the cups back on the tray. "You never know what you're going to get at the station, so I just started taking it black for simplicity."

"That makes sense."

"But thank you." It was sweet. It was beyond sweet. She waited until he'd returned the tray of unused milks to the lady behind the counter, who didn't look entirely impressed to take them back. "How about you?" she asked when he sat down. "Sugar?"

Aiden laughed. "No way. I'm like you." He lifted his cup. "I drink it black because I need it strong to deal with teenagers all day. But I do put a splash of cold water in the first cup each morning."

"Water?"

He shrugged. "I guess I'm just impatient for that first cup. The water cools it down just enough to start drinking immediately so I can get that caffeine hit."

"To deal with the teenagers?"

He pointed one finger at her and smiled. "Exactly."

"They can't be that bad, are they?"

For Natalie, it sounded like a specific kind of torture to have to spend her days in a high school surrounded by teenagers, but thankfully for society, there were some people—like Aiden—who enjoyed that kind of thing.

"Not at all." Aiden took a sip of his coffee. "I love the kids. For the most part," he added quickly. "But they are really great."

She pressed her lips together.

"You don't think so?" He frowned. "Were they jerks to you in class the other day, or—"

"Oh goodness, no," Natalie said quickly. "Your class was great." Reflecting back on it, they had been kind of great kids. Sure, they were loud and rowdy at the beginning of class, but once she'd started teaching, they'd all responded to her and the first-aid techniques really well. Natalie hadn't even let herself think about it, but for how worked up she'd been about setting foot in the school, her actual experience had been pretty positive. "I actually really enjoyed it," she answered honestly.

"You sound surprised."

"I am," she answered said. "I didn't have the best experience in high school and I guess…well, it doesn't matter."

The last thing she wanted to talk to Aiden about on their first *coffee* was how she'd been the most unpopular person in school. That was definitely not the way to set the tone with a man who was no doubt the most popular guy in school. How could he not be? With a sexy smile like that, no doubt he'd had the girls lined up around the block. Maybe he was even one of those guys who dated *all* the girls. And like Brandon Ryan, had made it a point to *sleep* with all of the girls. Or, when the girl said no, *tell* everyone he'd slept with her and that she was a total slut.

The coffee soured in Natalie's stomach and she pushed away the plate with the honey bun.

"Are you okay? You look…"

"I'm fine." She nodded but she was anything *but* fine. She hadn't thought about Brandon Ryan and the rumors that had ruined her life in *years*. And then the moment she stepped foot in the high school, it had all come back. It was ridiculous. All of those old feelings had no place in her brain anymore. Especially now, when she was sitting with a gorgeous man who was actually interested in her.

"Are you sure?" Aiden had jumped up from his seat. "Let me get you some water."

While he was gone, Natalie used the opportunity to take a few deep breaths and pull herself together.

You are not that girl anymore.

You are not in high school.

You are a strong, confident woman.

That is all in the past.

By the time Aiden returned to the table, Natalie once more had herself under control. She accepted the glass of water from him with an embarrassed smile. "I'm sorry," she said. "I don't know what happened there, but…"

"Don't worry about it. I have that effect on women sometimes."

She choked on the water in her mouth and had to reach for a napkin to keep from spitting it out on the table, and Aiden. He laughed as she wiped at her face. "Oh my goodness, I'm sorry. You just…"

"I also have *that* effect on women."

He definitely had some kind of effect on women. At least, he did on her. And for the life of her, Natalie couldn't decide whether that was a good thing or not.

Aiden couldn't remember the last time he'd enjoyed himself so much.

Spending time with Natalie was easy.

Their conversation had flowed and with the exception of one moment when he'd been sure he'd said something wrong that had put her off, everything had gone perfectly. Even that moment, when she'd seemed to have gone off in her own thoughts, had passed quickly and it hadn't taken long for them to get right back on track. He wanted to see more of her. A lot more.

But when they'd finished their coffee and honey buns, and Natalie told him she had more errands to run before her shift started at the station house, Aiden had reluctantly agreed to part ways for the day. After all, every minute he'd spent away from his kitchen table and the piles and piles of unmarked papers he had to make his way through before Monday meant another minute he'd be up into the wee hours of the morning.

His workload certainly wasn't decreasing by spending time with Natalie.

But for the first time in his teaching career, he didn't care. Something felt more important than the work that waited for him.

Still. He had to be responsible, and the kids were depending on him getting their marks back to them in a timely fashion. So, after reluctantly saying good-bye to Natalie, with the promise of her not backing out of their hike on Tuesday, he ordered another coffee to go and headed home to start marking.

Aiden was about halfway through the pile when his phone rang.

He grabbed it without looking at the caller ID. A move he regretted the second he heard her voice.

"Aiden, thank God."

Brenna.

Shit.

It wasn't the end of the month. He hadn't missed a payment. But still, he knew exactly why she was calling.

"Hi, Brenna. What's going—"

"I'm so glad you answered your phone. I've been thinking about all the things you could be doing and where you might be and—"

"You know where I am, Brenna. I told you I moved to Glacier Falls in time to start the fall semester." He tried to keep his annoyance at bay. It was all part of Brenna's act. She liked to play the victim. An innocent who needed as much help as possible. Which turned out to be *a lot.* It was an act he'd fallen for once. Okay, more than once. And by the time he'd woken up to who Brenna really was, a lazy woman-child who'd rather play games and manipulate other people than do anything for herself, they'd already been married six months.

He still didn't know how she'd done it, but for a woman who spent her whole life trying to do as little as possible, Brenna had gone to work when it came to their divorce. Despite their short marriage, somehow she'd managed to wrangle a ridiculous amount of spousal support from him that he had to pay her monthly, for two years. A term he could have fought harder against. But at the time, Aiden just wanted to be done and put that chapter of his life behind him. It didn't do much for a man's self-esteem to have a constant reminder of his own poor choices around.

Besides, he'd reasoned that two years would go by quickly and it had. He only had one more payment left in their agreement and then he'd be free from her forever.

Which was exactly why she was calling now.

No doubt, Brenna had spent the last two years trying to line up her next meal ticket—aka an unsuspecting man who couldn't see past her bright-blue eyes, sinful smile, and equally sinful curves that had been the source of all his poor decisions.

But if she was calling him now, it was because she either hadn't secured her plan B, or she was just getting greedy.

Either way, Aiden didn't want anything to do with it.

"I know you ran away to the mountains," she crooned, her voice dripping with insincerity. "I bet you're doing the whole sexy mountain man thing, aren't you?"

"What's up, Brenna?" He refused to engage. "I'm working. I need to—"

"Working? On a Saturday? You work too hard, baby."

"Not your baby."

Dammit. He was falling into her trap.

"You know you'll always be my—"

"Seriously." He needed to get her off the phone. "What can I do for you? I need to get back to work."

"Fine." Her voice was clipped. Her attitude shifted quickly and dramatically. "I need to extend our agreement."

"No."

"Aiden."

"No, Brenna." He shook his head. He wouldn't fall for it. "It's over. The last payment will be in your account next month and then we're done. It's what we agreed on."

"We didn't agree, Aiden. It's not fair that you make so much money and I'm over here living in—"

"You are kidding, right?" Aiden forced himself to take a deep breath and release it slowly before continuing. "Sorry, Brenna. I can't help you. Take care."

He hung up the phone and flipped it to silent before dropping his chin to his chest.

One more month. One more month.

That was it. One more payment he could barely afford on his meager salary, and then he was done. He'd made the cross-country move to Glacier Falls not only for the mountains and the lifestyle options, but mostly to put distance between himself and his past life. Brenna represented all of the things he wasn't anymore: shallow, focused on appearances. A moron.

Because only a moron would let himself fall for her act the way he had.

He reached his arm around his back and massaged his tense shoulder muscles. One bad decision, no matter how bad it was, didn't define you. He knew that. He also knew that he couldn't be personally responsible for Brenna forever. He'd done more than his share. Sure, he'd married her when he never should have. He owned that. And he'd paid for it. Now it was time to move on. And as soon as that last payment came out of his bank account, he could finally officially do that.

He'd waited two long years, almost as a penance for his poor choices, to date again. And he'd needed that time to figure things out for himself. Because no matter what, he was not going to make the same mistakes a second time around. It wasn't only two years of penance and a sabbatical from dating; it was learning what he wanted and what he didn't want. Mostly what he *didn't* want, which was a liar. Brenna had proved to be a liar at every turn. Some big. Some small. All lies. She'd told him her mother had passed away—she lived two towns over but they didn't get along. She would fail to tell him where she was going, or who she was out with—usually other men—and then insist that a *lie by omission* wasn't a thing.

It got to the point where he couldn't believe a word she said. It was a terrible way to live. Which was why he needed a woman who would be one hundred percent honest. Always.

He'd given himself two years. And now, time was up.

And the timing couldn't be more perfect.

The vision of Natalie's genuine, bright smile filled his mind.

Aiden got up from the table and stretched his arms over his head as he walked to the living room window and looked out. He'd been lucky to find a rental he could afford. Lucky for him, the timing had been perfect for Brody Morris, too—the head chef and owner of Birchwood, the restaurant in town. He'd recently gotten married and moved into Sarah's home with her and her daughter, leaving his house vacant.

Maybe he could take Natalie to Birchwood on a proper date?

Yes.

Coffee had been great. And he was sure that the hike in a few days would be fun, too. Because so far, every second he spent with Natalie was fantastic. But a real date with her? One where they dressed up, and he took her for a nice dinner, and they learned more about each other before he walked her to her door at the end of the night and leaned in for a kiss on those sweet lips that were sure to be as soft as they looked…oh yes.

A real date with Natalie sounded like the perfect way to move on.

Chapter Six

ULTIMATELY, it didn't matter how excited Natalie had been for a winter hike that she was not remotely prepared for, because Mother Nature had other plans. The weather system that had brought a few feet of fresh snow had moved in late Monday afternoon and stayed for most of the next few days. Not only had it taken the hike completely off the table for Aiden's Outdoor Ed class, but it had also meant that her shifts had been busy.

A winter snowstorm in the mountains meant lots of car accident callouts, most of which weren't serious, fortunately. And there had also been two calls for smoke concerns with fireplaces that hadn't been properly maintained, and one actual fire that had been confined to a garage but had only left the homeowners shaken, and rightly so.

No matter how many times Natalie was in a fire, she didn't get used to it and she didn't think she ever would.

It had been a long week. But even though she was completely exhausted and the idea of crawling into her bed with a glass of wine and a good show on Netflix sounded like the perfect way to spend her day off, one other thing sounded even better.

Teaching first aid to a bunch of high schoolers.

She couldn't help but laugh at herself.

Was it only just a short week ago that she'd been petrified to set foot inside the building at all? And now she was actually looking forward to it?

Things changed.

And her change in attitude had nothing to do with the actual students or the school itself, but everything to do with the sexy teacher with the smoldering eyes who would be leading that class. And, well, maybe the students weren't too bad either.

Aiden was waiting for her in the parking lot when she pulled up. His face split into a broad smile when he saw her. She lifted her fingers in a wave and hopped out of the truck.

"Were you waiting for me?"

"I was." He moved in and for a hopeful minute, Natalie thought he might hug her. To her sharp disappointment, he stopped short of the hug but stood close enough that she could smell the hint of peppermint on his breath.

Had he popped a breath mint for her?

The thought made her smile even more. If it were possible.

Natalie had hardly stopped smiling since their impromptu coffee the weekend before and every time she thought about Aiden, her entire body warmed and the smile couldn't be stopped. If she didn't know better, she'd think she was falling for him.

But then again, why not? And why shouldn't she?

"I thought you might need a little help with your stuff," Aiden said. "We're going to be using the CPR dummies today, right?"

"You are right." She cringed inwardly at the thought of

babysitting a room full of teenagers with the CPR dummies. But then again, they might surprise her.

"Don't worry," Aiden said, reading her thoughts. "The kids are excited for today and they're really willing to learn. There shouldn't be too much inappropriate behavior with the dummies. I mean…" He wiggled his hand side to side. "There will definitely be some because…teenage boys."

She laughed.

"But honestly," Aiden continued. "They are really looking forward to today's class. When the hike was cancelled—"

"Which sucks, by the way. I was looking forward to it."

"So was I." He nodded slightly. "We'll definitely have to try for another time."

"Yes." Natalie realized belatedly that she'd interrupted him. "Sorry. I didn't mean to interrupt. You were telling me how excited the kids are to learn first aid because I'm such a great teacher." She winked and handed him CPR dummies from the back of the truck as they spoke.

"You are." With both of them loaded up with equipment, they headed into the school. "And I hope that means you've looked into those wilderness survival classes, too. Because I think you'd be perfect to teach them."

She looked over her stack of dummies at him, but he wasn't watching her. Instead, he was trying to navigate the front door with everything he was holding.

"Besides," he said a few minutes later, once they were both in the gym and had divested themselves of the loads they were carrying. "It would mean that we could spent a lot more time together."

Natalie jerked her head up to see him grinning at her. But before she could respond, the bell rang and students poured into the gym, just as Aiden said, eager for class to start. He winked at her and turned to greet the kids.

To say she was inexperienced when it came to flirting was a massive understatement, but even not knowing anything about anything, Natalie knew that wink meant something.

And she was excited to see exactly what that was.

"Mr. Adams, look!"

"Mr. Adams!"

"Check this out, Mr. Adams!"

Aiden loved it when his students were engaged in what they were learning. Even if it meant being pulled in a dozen directions at the same time because they were keen to show him the skills they'd learned. And he couldn't help but be impressed. The kids had really picked up quite a few first aid skills in only a few short classes. He stopped to survey the room with satisfaction. This was why he'd gotten into teaching. To make a difference and spark the love for learning.

Now if only he could do that with the same success rate in his English classroom, then he'd really be getting somewhere. Maybe he should get Natalie to come and teach a class in there, as well?

It wasn't a bad idea.

Especially because it would mean spending even more time with her, which was all he really wanted to do. When he wasn't with her, he was thinking about her. *Was she working? Was she having a good day? Would she like to go out with him?*

It was ridiculous. Never before had a woman had this kind of effect on him. He hardly knew her, and yet…maybe that was the problem? Maybe he just needed to get to know her better so that he could stop obsessing about her so much.

But even as the thought formulated, he dismissed it. Aiden knew instinctively that the more he learned about Natalie

Collins, the more he was going to want to know. It would be a vicious circle. And one he was a thousand percent interested in getting caught up in.

"Thanks again," Aiden said when the class ended and the last of the straggling students had left. "The kids really respond to you. Are you sure you never wanted to be a high school teacher? It's like you were born to do this."

The sound that came out of her mouth was a combination of a laugh and a snort. She quickly clamped a hand over her mouth. "Sorry. I don't mean to laugh." She shrugged. "Okay, well, maybe I did. The idea of me being a teacher is pretty hilarious."

"Why is that? You're genuinely good at it."

"Because to be a teacher," she started, "and a high school teacher specifically…" She looked over her shoulder a little before turning back to him and continuing. "You have to be in a high school."

He didn't get it. Aiden shook his head in confusion. "But you're *in* a high school right now."

"True." Natalie reached past him to grab the leftover first-aid manuals.

Her arm brushed his and the innocent touch sparked a flood of images in his brain that were far from innocent. He forced himself to focus on what she was saying.

"Up until last week," she said, "I swore I'd never set foot in another high school again." She looked him straight in the eyes. "Ever."

"Ahh. Because you didn't have a good time in high school." He remembered when she'd mentioned that."

She pointed a finger at him. "Nailed it."

"I know you said that, but…you have *no* good memories? What about a school dance? Everyone has a good dance experience."

She laughed hard but there was no humor in it. "*Especially* not a dance." She shook her head. "Without going into details, let's just say my high school experience was probably the exact opposite of yours."

He shook his head. "It just doesn't make any sense, though."

"Why is that?" She crossed her arms over her chest, pushing her breasts up and together in a way that strained the T-shirt she wore.

Aiden was positive that she had no idea she was doing it, but the simple action had his heart racing. And if he wasn't careful, other parts of his body would be reacting in a moment, too.

"Is it because I'm blonde?" she asked. "I mean, I look like—"

"A cheerleader," he finished for her. Damn, if she'd been a cheerleader at one of his hockey games when he was younger, he would have been in trouble. The fact that they didn't have cheerleaders at hockey games didn't seem to matter. "But no," he said quickly. "I mean, yes. You look like you could have been a cheerleader, but that's not what I meant. I mean, just because you're blonde and beautiful, it doesn't guarantee that your high school experience will be a good one." He shrugged. "I've been a teacher long enough to know that it's hard for everyone from time to time. And…well, I guess…I'm sorry."

"You're sorry?" She tilted her head in question. "What are you sorry for? It wasn't your fault high school was awful for me. We didn't even know each other."

But maybe if they had…

It was a ridiculous thought. Still, something about Natalie made him want to fix things for her. Not that she needed him to fix anything, but if he could…he would.

"I don't know," he tried to explain. "I guess, as a teacher myself and a kid who mostly had a good school experience, I feel like it's my duty to change your mind about how great high school can be."

She shook her head with a laugh. "I appreciate the sentiment, but I'd settle for a hand out to my truck with all this for today."

"You know," Natalie said when the last of the dummies were stowed carefully in the back of the truck, "this was actually a lot of fun. And even though I don't have a lot of positive things to say about my own high school experience, I think it could have been different if I'd gone to school with kids like your students. They're actually pretty great."

She saw the way Aiden pulled his shoulders back a little and how his smile grew even broader on his handsome face. He cared about his students. It was clear to see. As was the pride he had in them.

"They're awesome kids," he agreed. "I'm pretty lucky to be their teacher."

"Wow."

"What?" He crossed his arms, a simple move that directed all of her focus and attention to his biceps that strained against his cotton button-down shirt. Despite the brisk day, he hadn't worn a jacket outside, but he didn't seem bothered by the cold.

It was a small detail, but one Natalie couldn't help but be grateful for because, as much as she knew she probably shouldn't, she couldn't help but stare at him. Aiden had the body of an athlete. There didn't seem to be an ounce of unnecessary flesh on him. Even fully clothed—*whoa*. Where had that thought come from? As if he would ever *not* be fully clothed around her. That would imply…what? What would that imply?

That she wanted him? That she was incredibly attracted to

him in a way that she could honestly say she'd *never* been before? In fact, Natalie had *never* had such—I-hardly-know-you-but-I-could-rip-your-clothes-off-right-now—feelings before. *Ever.*

"Nothing," she said quickly as she blew out the air in her lungs and had to look away. "It's just..." She turned back to him and looked him straight in his dark coffee-colored eyes that took her breath away. "You do know how lucky those kids are to have you, right?"

It wasn't her imagination that the tips of his ears darkened with the compliment. She'd embarrassed him. But nothing she'd said wasn't true.

"Well," Aiden said after a moment. "I appreciate the compliment."

They stood in silence for what was dangerously approaching an awkward moment. Natalie needed to get going. She still had to return the dummies to the station house before running home for a quick shower and change. Katie Banks had invited her out for a girls night at the local pub and she was ridiculously excited—and equally nervous about it. But still, she didn't want to leave Aiden.

There was a pull to be with him, and it only grew stronger every time they were together. Natalie didn't even know how to begin explaining it because she'd never felt anything like it before. All she really knew was that when she spent time with him, she never wanted it to end.

"Would you like to go for dinner at Birchwood? Tomorrow night? About seven?" She blurted out the question before she'd even realized she had.

Had she seriously just asked him out? Just like that?

Surprised by herself, Natalie instinctively opened her mouth to rescind the invitation, but changed her mind and with confidence she never would have had ten years ago, added, "Like a date?"

He took a step backward, obviously taken a little off guard with her forward offer. "A date?"

She nodded. "Yes. A date. With me." She was in it now. If he said no, she'd...well...

"I can't think of anything I'd like more."

Natalie released the breath she'd been holding and laughed. "I thought you might say no."

Aiden's eyes widened and he reached for her arm. His touch was light, but her skin heated under his fingers. "You're kidding, right?"

She shook her head.

"I can't wait to take you out for dinner."

She opened her mouth to protest. After all, she'd asked *him* out.

"And yes," he said before she could disagree. "I would really like to take you out. Because you beat me to it. I was just about to ask you."

"That's not true."

"Of course it is." He moved closer, his hand still on her arm. "Natalie, I've been dying to ask you out almost from the moment I heard you whistle in that gymnasium."

She dropped her head back in laughter. When she looked up again, Aiden was looking at her with such intensity her breath hitched.

He was close. Closer than a man had ever been. And she liked it. A lot. She wanted him closer.

Instinctively, she leaned forward to close the small amount of space between them. She'd been bold asking him out. *Could she be even bolder and kiss—*

"Mr. Adams!"

Aiden took a very big and very quick step backward, putting space between them as two students rushed over to them.

"Mr. Adams, I need an extension on my paper. I can't get it done tonight and if I fail, I can't play in the game next week."

Aiden gave her an apologetic shrug but she couldn't be upset, because she'd meant what she'd said earlier—those kids were lucky to have him as a teacher.

Besides, she thought as she drove away, it was pretty damn sexy to see the way he cared about his job and definitely one of the things that was making her fall for him.

Natalie was still thinking about Aiden a few hours later when she joined Katie for girls drinks at the local pub and favorite hangout. Katie had waved her over the moment she'd set foot inside the dimly lit room and introduced her to Sarah Morris before ordering drinks.

"It's going to be a smaller group tonight," Katie said. "But I think Faith will be here in a bit. You've met Faith, right?"

"I sort of met a lot of people in passing at the Christmas Eve event at the fire hall," Natalie said. "But I'm really looking forward to actually getting to know people better because I don't think that really counted since I was busy slicing turkey all night."

"Jeremy totally made you do all the hard work, didn't he?" Katie laughed. "Jeremy and I are old friends. I remember when he was the rookie and had to do all the grunt work himself."

"It's all part of it, I guess. And I don't mind." She accepted the drink the waitress handed her. "In fact, as the rookie, I actually got to teach the first-aid class at the high school." It wasn't lost on her how just a few weeks ago, Natalie thought that was the worst thing she could be assigned to do. Funny how one sexy man with dreamy eyes could change her perspective.

"And that's how you met Aiden." Katie grinned. "Too bad about the hike."

Natalie nodded and was about to take a sip of her drink, when Sarah added, "But dinner at Birchwood will be so much better anyway."

Her eyebrows shot up and Natalie put the drink down before she could spill it. "What?"

"You are going to Birchwood tomorrow night?" Sarah asked with a sly smile. "On a date, right?"

Natalie looked between the other women. "How...but..."

"How did I know?"

"Yes? How did you know? I mean..." It was only a few hours ago that she'd even asked him. How was it possible that people—people she didn't even know—knew about her *date*?

"Small town." Katie laughed.

"And, my husband is Brody," Sarah said with a shake of her head. "He's the owner at Birchwood and, we're renting his house to Aiden."

"Oh, that...doesn't help." Natalie laughed a little, still confused. Maybe she'd have to get used to the whole living in a small town, where everyone knew everyone's business thing. But this was fast, even for a small town.

"Well, to be fair," Sarah added, "Aiden called Brody a few hours ago and asked to reserve the best table." Sarah clawed a hand over her mouth. "Which I probably shouldn't be telling you because it's supposed to be a surprise." Her eyes widened as she realized what she'd done. "I'm so sorry, Natalie. I—"

"It's fine. Besides, I asked him out—shouldn't I be making the reservations?" She hadn't even thought about that, and secretly she was glad that Aiden had taken charge if it meant getting a good table at the best restaurant in town.

"Well, either way, you're going on a date with that sexy teacher." Katie wiggled her shoulders in a little dance. "And really, that man is *so* into you, Nat." She turned to Sarah. "You should see it, Sarah. Their connection is *fire*. I mean, really. He looks at her like he's going to eat her up. It's awesome."

Eat her up? Katie was just being dramatic, but still, it had put an image in Natalie's head that she wasn't sure she wanted to let go of. Was their attraction to each other really that obvious? Was Aiden *really* that in to her?

He'd been about to kiss her earlier, hadn't he?

A shiver ran through her. The idea of kissing him or eventually doing more with Aiden both excited her, and terrified her. *Would she know what to do? What if she did it wrong?* It was ludicrous that an almost twenty-eight-year-old woman didn't know how to kiss a man. She looked at the other women, who had dissolved into an easy conversation about their husbands.

Should she tell the truth to her new friends? Would they have some good advice for her?

Could she trust them?

That was the real question. It had been a *very* long time since Natalie had female friends. Not good ones, anyway. And definitely not the type of friends who she would admit such a thing to. But Sarah and Katie were different.

Still, the last thing she wanted was for them to make fun of her or think she was a weirdo because she was still a virgin and had never even had a real kiss. But even more powerful was her desire to not screw things up with Aiden. Maybe it wouldn't be a bad idea to get a little female advice.

"Hey," she spoke up, interrupting them. "Can I tell you guys—"

"Ladies! I made it."

Before Natalie could admit her secret, they were joined at the table by Faith Langdon and her cell phone. "And look who I brought." Faith took a seat. "Sort of."

"Hi, ladies." Stephanie Starz waved from the screen. "I wish I could be there with you all."

Faith moved the phone around so they could all say hi in turn.

When it was Natalie's turn, she lifted her fingers in a shy wave, doubtful that Stephanie even knew who she was.

"Stop!" Stephanie commanded from the phone. "Natalie? Is that you?"

Chapter Seven

SHE WOULD WAY RATHER BE THERE in person, but through the power of technology, Steph would settle for a virtual girls night, even if it made Faith crazy. Her poor sister had been putting up with her for over an hour already, as their video chat had started at Ever After Ranch and a visit with Hope and the baby, who had just come home. When Steph heard that Cole was given the green light to go home with an oxygen tank, she'd almost flown home at once to be there for the occasion.

It was her agent Lewis who talked sense into her. Shooting on her new film, *Bombshell*, had just begun. She was needed on set every day for the next week at least. And then, if it all went well, she'd get a small break to fly home and finally cuddle her nephew in her arms.

But until then, she had her other sister, who she was going to owe big time after all of Faith's indulging in Steph's video chatting.

"Natalie?" The moment the phone panned over to the blonde at the end of the table, Steph shrieked, unable to contain her excitement. "Is that you?"

The other woman blushed, and Stephanie felt a little bad for putting her on the spot.

Natalie waved her fingers. "Hi."

"Oh, I wish I was there to give you a hug." Steph bounced up and down and called over her shoulder. "Bella, it's Natalie!"

"Is Bella there?" Katie asked from somewhere outside the video frame. "I want to say hi."

A moment later, Bella, who was sharing a condo in Los Angeles with Steph, popped her head down next to her and waved. "I can't talk long. I need to go chat with Jeremy. But hi all. I miss you, girls!"

Bella blew a kiss to the screen and then was gone again.

Steph knew she had her own video chat with her fiancé, Jeremy, to get to. They were religious about making time for each other, which was probably a good thing because in Steph's experience, relationships in show business were hard. *Very* hard. But Jeremy and Bella seemed determined to make a go of it. And if anyone had a chance, it was the two of them. Their love for each other was inspiring.

"Natalie," Steph put the attention back on the firefighter, "I can't thank you enough."

"All of us," Faith said from behind the camera. "It was all so incredible, Nat. Seriously."

Steph nodded. "I'm so glad you were there, Natalie. We'll celebrate when I get back there, okay?"

The other woman nodded, clearly uncomfortable with the attention. "I'm just glad mom and baby are doing well."

"Show us pictures!" Sarah demanded off-camera.

A moment later, Faith flipped the phone around so she was staring at her sister. "The ladies want pictures, sis. I gotta let you go."

Steph smiled. Despite her disappointment, she understood. It had been so long since she'd felt such a sense of belonging the way she did in Glacier Falls, with all of the people there, that it made her heart ache to be away. But it was only temporary. As soon as filming was done, she'd be back. It was a balancing act between the career she loved and the new home she was falling in love with a little more each day.

"I get it." She blew Faith a kiss. "Thank you for being my eyes. Love you, sis."

"Talk soon." Faith blew a kiss back and then, she was gone.

The screen went blank. Steph stared at the dark screen for a second and was just about to tuck her phone away and pick up her script when it lit up again with an incoming call.

"Nick!" She answered the video call. "I just got off with Faith and the girls. What a nice surprise. What are you up to?"

"Packing." Her friend's handsome face filled the screen. His eyes, framed by his signature thick black frames, looked tired and his dark hair stood up oddly in the front, but he looked good. Happy. Being a new father, no matter how it had come to be for him, suited him. "We're moving in a few weeks."

"I'm so happy you decided to go back to Glacier Falls."

"Well, it's not like I was ever really *there*," he said with a bashful grin.

It was true. Nick Newton had only ever visited Glacier Falls, even if it had turned into an extended visit after coming to town for Damon's wedding to Katie. Together, Nick and Damon had invented some sort of microchip that Steph didn't fully understand, before selling it for millions of dollars. The two of them were ridiculously wealthy, but also some of the nicest men Steph had ever met. Wealthy or not.

For a time, Steph had wondered whether maybe something could work out with her and Nick. But as much as she liked him and enjoyed spending time with him, there was no spark and they'd settled into an easy and solid friendship.

"Still," she said. "I'm really happy you're going back. Glacier Falls will be the perfect place for you to raise Amelia."

His smile dipped a little and he ran a hand through his hair, making it stand up in entirely different directions.

"What?" Concern for her friend filled her. "What's going on?"

"It's nothing." He shook his head. "Really. I'm not going to worry about anything until there's something to worry about. Besides, that's not why I'm calling."

Steph knew that she could push him on it, but she wouldn't get anywhere. Nick was stubborn. It was part of what had made him so successful in his line of work. He knew when to lock in and once he decided on something, there was no point pushing it. "What?" she teased. "You didn't call to see my beautiful face?"

He laughed. "You know I love seeing your beautiful face. But no, that's not it either."

"Whatever it is you need, you know I'll help."

"I do," he said with a nod. "Which is why I wanted to ask you about the guest house at ElkView Ridge."

"The guest house?" She sat back with surprise. "Damon and Katie's guest house?"

Why would Nick want to ask her about their friends' guest house? It's not like she—*ah*. Steph laughed with understanding the moment it all made sense. "I'm guessing you were hoping to move into the guest house at ElkView?"

He didn't hesitate to nod. "Not forever. Just until the renovations on the new place are done. I found a great spot right in town, but it needed a little updating."

Of course it did.

"And I know you're out of town working, and I was just—"

"Of course." Steph didn't hesitate to give her answer. If it meant that Nick moved to Glacier Falls with his sweet baby sooner, rather than waiting, she'd do anything. Nick was a great guy, and he was doing an amazing job as a single dad, particularly when the whole situation had caught him off guard and he was almost positive that he was not Amelia's father. But he still needed help and support, and he'd have that in Glacier Falls.

"You should move in," she said. "And you're right, I'm not even going to be there much."

Not much. But some.

With the Big Rock Inn lost in a recent fire, and the cabins at Lynx Creek not near completion yet, she really didn't have a lot of options as far as where to stay when she went to visit. And she *would* be going to visit. How could she not with now not one, but two babies who needed her cuddles?

"Thanks, Steph." Nick was talking, but Steph was only half listening. "And if you need a place when you come to town, you know I'll always make room for you."

He wiggled his eyebrows, and Steph couldn't help but burst out laughing.

After signing off with Nick, Steph poured herself a glass of wine and moved outside to the deck by the pool. The end of February, it was still cool, even in Los Angeles, but it was a lot warmer than back home. She wrapped a throw blanket around her legs and stared into the blue water, lit by the underwater lights.

It was a nice house. Nothing too flashy, but big enough for both Steph and Bella. And, of course, Jeremy when he came to visit. And sure, she could have rented a place by herself, but more and more, Steph was enjoying being with people. With *family.* And even though Bella wasn't blood related, she'd become a fast friend. And someone Stephanie definitely considered part of her family. Besides, if she could help her friend, who was new to the world of Hollywood, navigate what could be the somewhat turbulent waters of becoming a massive star, she wanted to do what she could to help. It wasn't easy.

"Hey. Am I interrupting?" Bella, along with the bottle of wine in her hand, sat on the chair next to her.

"Not at all. I was just thinking." Steph smiled and returned to gazing over the pool.

"About anything in particular?" Bella took a sip of her wine and sighed as she reclined into the chair. "This is lovely."

"It *is* lovely."

"So," Bella pushed, "what are you thinking about?"

Steph looked at her new friend. Bella's shiny dark hair hung over her shoulders in waves. Even in sweatpants and a T-shirt, she was beautiful. A *bombshell*. Which was exactly what she was. With her voice, and that gorgeous face, never mind her sweet, down-to-earth personality, she was going to be a massive star. She didn't even fully understand it yet, but her entire life was about to change when this movie was released.

"I was just thinking how things always seem to have a way of working out the way they're supposed to."

"That's a very deep thought for a random Thursday night." Bella raised her eyebrows and took a sip of her wine. "Is there anything in particular you're hoping will work out?"

"Oh no." Steph laughed. "It's not that I'm *hoping* it will work out. I'm just saying, I know it will." She pulled her phone out from where she'd stashed it under her leg.

"How can you *know* that? I mean, it's one thing to hope and want things to work out, but I don't think we can ever *know* that it will all work out the way we want to," Bella said seriously as she considered what Steph was saying. "No one can actually *know* it, though."

Steph held out her phone and wiggled it. "Well, from my experience, there's one way to move things along in your favor." She unlocked the screen and opened up her text messages, scrolling until she found the name and number she was looking for. She quickly typed a message.

Timeline is moving up. When can you have the bankside cabin ready?

She grinned at Bella before hitting the Send button. "You just have to ask."

Chapter Eight

"THIS IS AMAZING, AIDEN."

Natalie put another bite of the halibut in her mouth and closed her eyes, just as she had every bite previously. To say it was distracting to watch her eat would be putting it mildly. Aiden fought a constant and continuous war within himself every single time he saw her do that.

Not that he was going to look away.

Hell no.

Watching how much Natalie enjoyed her food had been a highlight of their date. So far. And only one of many.

Pretty much the entire evening had been awesome. Conversation had flowed; they'd laughed and gotten to know each other far more than just the high school teacher and the firefighter who taught first aid. It had been perfect.

"I can't even tell you how glad I am that you're enjoying it, Natalie. Really." Aiden used his fork to break a piece of his own fish off, and took a bite. "I think Brody outdid himself this time."

"It was really sweet of you to request a special meal." She set her fork down as she spoke, a fact he was grateful for only because maybe for a small second he could stop thinking sexy thoughts about her. She smiled and dipped her head a bit so her blonde hair fell over her shoulder and between the cleavage of her dress.

So much for not thinking sexy thoughts.

Aiden took a long drink of water. If he thought Natalie was sexy as hell in her firefighter uniform, seeing her in a low-cut dress that showed off her breasts and hugged her curves was downright sinful. *He couldn't even imagine what she'd look like in only—*

No. He stopped himself from going down that particular line of thinking. There was no way he'd be able to finish his dinner if he started thinking of how gorgeous she would look with her skin flushed, panting with desire while he kissed every inch of—*fuck.*

Too late.

Thankfully, Natalie was still talking about the meal and how delicious it was. He forced himself to focus. He was never even going to get a first kiss if he made a complete and total fool of himself first, and he did *not* want to screw things up with Natalie. She was different and special. Strong and independent, she was smart and funny and absolutely everything he was looking for in a woman.

"It was my pleasure," he said. "I really wanted our first date to be special."

"Not fair." She picked up her wine but instead of taking a sip, she held it as she spoke. "I asked you out. I should have made the arrangements."

"It was merely a technicality." He put his fork down. He couldn't eat another bite. "You beat me by seconds. I was just about to ask you."

"That's not true." She laughed.

"You're right. I was actually about to kiss you."

Her laughter died as her skin flushed. She looked surprised

and embarrassed and so completely innocent all at once. It was incredibly sexy.

"Did you not want me to?"

She put her wine glass on the table and dropped her gaze to her plate before answering. "No." She shook her head and looked up. "I did want you to."

Aiden couldn't have stopped the grin on his face if he'd wanted to. And he didn't.

This woman. She was full of surprises, and he wanted to discover all of them.

He took a chance—because, hell, why not?—and reached across the table to take her hand. She didn't pull away, so Aiden slowly turned her hand in his until her palm faced up. He stroked the soft skin, just a little, and looked into her eyes.

"I'm really happy to hear that."

"I'm sorry to interrupt." The waiter, who didn't seem all that sorry to interrupt at all, ruined the moment, and Natalie pulled her hand away. "Are you all done here?"

They nodded, and he cleared the plates away before once again reappearing to top up their wine glasses with the remainder of the bottle. "Can I get you two anything else this evening?"

"I think—"

"We have a delicious chocolate mousse," he continued, as if Aiden hadn't spoken. "It's finished with a raspberry coulis." The waiter looked directly at Natalie, whose eyes were growing wider as he explained the desserts.

The waiter listed a few more things, each sounding more delicious than the last, before finally leaving them to make their decision.

"Well," Aiden said. "They all sounded pretty amazing. Are you a dessert kind of woman?"

"You know what?" Her tongue peeked out between her lips just a little. "I usually would be a complete sucker for that mousse, but I don't think I could eat another bite right now."

"Another time, then?"

She smiled and nodded. "I'd really like that. But you know…" Her smile dipped a little at the corner. "I don't know if I'm ready for our evening to end, either."

Heat flared deep in Aiden's groin. *Was she suggesting what he hoped she was suggesting?* Damn. He wasn't usually one to fool around on a first date. But he also wasn't one to be so insanely attracted to a woman on a first date and if she wanted to—

"Would you be up for grabbing a coffee somewhere?"

Coffee. Yes. If she wanted a coffee, he'd have coffee with her. For sure. Hell, he'd even make her the best coffee she'd ever had.

"I would love that. But on one condition."

She tilted her head so that her silky blonde hair slipped from her shoulders.

"Let me make it for you. I have a very fancy espresso machine. I know you take it black, but if I can talk you into a latte or a cappuccino, it will change your life."

She laughed, but he didn't miss the hesitation in her eyes. "Change my life, huh?"

"You know it. Will you give me a chance?"

She'd give him a chance. Of course she would. But *his* house? Coffee?

It sounded innocent enough. Natalie might be totally and completely inexperienced, but she wasn't stupid. She knew what *coffee at his place* meant.

And she also knew she wasn't ready.

Was she?

To be fair, she had no idea what she was ready for or not.

She liked Aiden, a lot, and their dinner date had just made that even clearer. He was funny and a great storyteller. More than once, he'd branched off into stories about *his kids*. They clearly mattered a lot to him, and the passion he had for teaching was incredibly sexy.

It was just one of the many things about Aiden that was sexy, of course. But it was definitely another thing for an already growing list.

But back to his house? Alone?

She...found herself nodding and then heard her voice say, "Sounds great."

And it did. Sound great. *But also...*

She put a smile on her face and, not for the first time since things had started heating up with Aiden, she wished she had someone she could talk to about it. Someone who might be able to give her some advice. A friend. A *girlfriend.*

"Would you excuse me for a second?" Natalie grabbed her purse from the back of her chair as Aiden stood. "I just need to use the restroom. I'll be back in a moment."

"Of course." He smiled.

And just as it always did, his smile caused a flash of electricity to flow through her. Only this time, the flash settled low in her belly and pulsed with need.

She moved quickly through the restaurant toward the restrooms. She didn't even see Sarah until she almost ran directly into her. "Oh, I'm sorry."

"Natalie. Hi." Sarah caught her with her hands on Natalie's forearms. "You look like you're in a hurry." Her eyes flicked over Natalie's shoulder. "Is everything okay? You're..."

"I'm fine. I'm just..."

Natalie barely knew Sarah. She'd only really had the chance to talk to her once, the night before. But it wasn't as if they were able to talk about anything that really mattered. Still, just like all the other women of Glacier Falls, Sarah was so different than the female friends she'd had before. It was as though she actually cared about her friends, and maybe that included Natalie, too? Ultimately, Natalie had nothing to lose by trying.

"You know what?" Natalie changed tack quickly. "Can I ask you a question? In private?"

"Of course." Sarah didn't even hesitate. "Let me just make sure Rory is okay in the kitchen. I don't want her getting in the way." She nodded toward the ladies' room. "Give me five minutes."

It only took her two, and Sarah joined her in what could only be described as a cozy ladies' room. There was a sitting area off to the side of the sinks, with a tiny couch and a chair, potted plants and a table. Sarah walked in and handed Natalie a glass of wine, keeping one for herself. "I thought maybe you could use this."

"Thank you." Natalie took a small sip. She'd already had a glass and a half, and she definitely didn't want to drink too much, but at that moment, wine felt like a good fit. "I really appreciate you…well…talking to me, I guess."

Sarah laughed. "You do not have to thank me for that."

"It's just that I'm new to town, and I don't know—"

Sarah put a hand on her arm. "It doesn't matter if you're new or if you've been here your whole life. We've got you, Natalie. Let me tell you, this town and the people in it saved me when my first husband died."

Natalie sat back. She hadn't known that Sarah was married before. Sure, she'd known that her daughter was from a previous relationship, but…well, she hadn't really stopped to think about what that relationship was.

"Yes," Sarah said with a small smile. "I was married before and, without getting into too many details, Josh and I were high school sweethearts."

"I'm so sorry."

"It's fine." She nodded but to Nat's surprise, she didn't look sad. "It was a hard time for a lot of reasons," Sarah continued. "And I wanted to close myself up and hide from the world, but I didn't because—"

"Of your friends?"

"Exactly. And my point is, it's like that for everyone, Nat. You, too. You might be pretty new to town, but that doesn't matter. No matter what you need, we're here." She squeezed her arm to make her point. "Okay?"

Natalie nodded. "Okay."

"Great." Sarah sat up and sipped her own wine. "Now, tell me what is going on with you and that ridiculously sexy teacher out there, because from where I sit—not that I've been watching—he is crazy into you. I mean, in a huge way. Was dinner okay?"

"Dinner was delicious. So good."

"And now, let me guess, you're not sticking around for any of Birchwood's famous chocolate mousse, but opting for dessert of your own."

Natalie almost spat out the sip of wine she'd just taken. Instead, she managed to swallow it, but only just barely. "I…what…I…"

"Am I wrong?"

She wasn't. At least not really. Which was the whole problem.

The conflict must have shown on Natalie's face, because Sarah's smile faded and was instantly placed with a look of concern. "Oh. I…" She leaned forward. "Is that the problem?"

Natalie nodded. "I…this is so embarrassing, but…I've never…"

Sarah pressed her lips together and closed her eyes for a moment. "I get it." She put her wine glass down and leaned forward. "When I first met Brody and we…well, I hadn't been with anyone besides my husband and it was terrifying and…

exciting, too. I'm not going to pretend it's the same thing, but I will say this."

Natalie listened, grateful to have someone to talk to about it after all this time.

"There is no right or wrong answer," Sarah continued. "Whatever you do, just make sure you're more than comfortable with it, okay? Aiden seems like a good guy. He's not going to do anything you don't want to do."

Natalie nodded. She agreed with that. Aiden *was* a good guy and even though she didn't want to tell him that she was a virgin because it made her feel stupid and immature, she felt instinctively that he would understand *if* she did tell him.

"Go with your gut, Natalie, and you'll be okay."

"That's kind of vague advice, don't you think?" Natalie couldn't help but giggle a little.

"Sure it is." Sarah laughed. "But no one else can tell you what to do here. It's just about how you feel. I assume you have a reason for not…well, for saving yourself, and—"

"It's not like that." Natalie interrupted. "I mean, there's nothing wrong with saving yourself for marriage, but that's not why. I just…well, when I was young there was a—"

She stopped herself. It was one thing to have a quick girl chat in the ladies' room; it was a completely different thing to get into childhood trauma and drawn-out stories while your hot date, who you happened to be crazy attracted to, waited outside. "You know what?" She changed her mind. "That's a story for a different day. But the point of it is, I really like Aiden and I…well, I…"

"*Want* him."

She laughed. "I do."

"Well," Sarah stood, "then my best advice is to get back out there, and don't overthink anything. You're an adult. A strong, confident woman. You go do exactly what it is you want to, and don't let yourself get in your own way."

Natalie put her glass down and stood as well. She straightened her dress and pulled her shoulders back. "And that is the best advice I could have asked for. I think I'm going to do just that."

They'd walked hand in hand through the snowy streets to Brody's house just off Main Street, behind Birchwood. Natalie, as it turned out, lived within walking distance to Main Street as well, only in the opposite direction. She was in the new condos, overlooking the river. Either way, it was a small town and a nice night for walking, despite the snow. Having Natalie's hand in his made Aiden feel like a school kid again. He had butterflies in his stomach just thinking about kissing her for the first time.

When was the last time he'd had that feeling?

He couldn't remember. Too long. It had definitely been too long since he'd felt about a woman the way he was feeling about Natalie.

"This is me." Aiden guided her up the small walkway to the house he rented. He unlocked the door and flipped on the lights as he held the door for her.

She was nervous. It wasn't hard to see it. As soon as he'd suggested going back to his house for a coffee, something had shifted with her. She hadn't said no, but she'd become visibly edgy. As if she were unsure about him.

Or maybe she was hiding something.

No.

Aiden shot down the thought the second it entered his mind. He could not go through his life suspicious of every woman he met. Not everyone was like Brenna, operating with a hidden agenda. In fact, he needed to believe Brenna was the exception, not the rule. And Natalie was *nothing* like Brenna. She was just nervous. That was all.

"It's really nice." Natalie slipped off her coat and handed it to him before removing her boots. Somehow, in her stockinged feet, she seemed a little sweeter than before, if that was even possible.

"I can't take any credit for it." Aiden led her into the kitchen, where he fired up the espresso machine. "Almost everything in here is Brody's. He rented it to me fully furnished, including this bad boy." He waved his hand in a flourish over the shiny machine. "Can you grab two cups out of that cupboard over there while I—"

He grabbed a bag of beans, and almost spilled it as it slipped from his hands. He caught it just in time, thankfully, and Natalie laughed. It was a beautiful sound, because it meant she was starting to relax a little.

Now, if only he could do the same thing. But how? How could he relax with her in his kitchen, looking so sexy and so damn kissable and—he needed to get it out of the way. It was the only way he'd be able to function.

Aiden put the beans down next to the machine and crossed the room to where Natalie was reaching up into the cupboard to grab the cups he'd requested. He stood so close to her that the scent of the sweet jasmine perfume she wore filled his sinuses and almost rendered him useless.

Natalie must have been aware of his presence, because she stilled and then slowly turned around, one cup in her hand. "Did I get the wrong—"

"It's perfect." He took it from her hand and set it down next to her, moving him closer to her. "I...there's something that I've wanted to do for so long now, that I was thinking maybe we should just..." He slipped his hand to her cheek and cupped it gently.

She didn't close her eyes, holding his gaze instead, but her breath came faster, and her tongue slipped out, just a little to wet her lips.

Damn.

There was no doubt what it was Aiden wanted to do, and if he was any judge at all, it was clear that Natalie was looking forward to the kiss as much as he was. Still, he hesitated. "Natalie?" His voice was deep, just barely controlled. "Would it be okay if—"

Her lips, every bit as soft as he'd imagined, pressed to his before he could finish. And that was perfectly fine with him. Because the only thing that mattered was kissing her. Not *how* he was kissing her.

And damn, was he *ever* kissing her.

She was sweet, and spicy in a way he hadn't expected. Her kiss started off tentative and completely unsure, but in seconds, she seemed to have found her footing. She released the smallest moan against his lips, and the sound was almost Aiden's undoing.

His groin tightened and with one hand still on her cheek, he used the other hand to slide behind her hair into her silky locks and pull her toward him. He needed her closer. He needed her—

"Oh."

She pulled away and touched her fingers to her lips as if she could hardly believe she'd just done that.

Believe it! he wanted to yell. *Because if I have anything to say about it, we're going to be doing a whole lot more of that.*

"I...didn't...I mean...I did..." She giggled, and it was the most adorable thing he'd ever seen.

Especially because Natalie was gorgeous, strong, and beautiful. But adorable wouldn't have been one of the words he would have described her with.

Until now.

"I'm glad you did." Aiden shifted so he could reach out and brush a strand of hair from her cheek. "Even if you did beat me to it, again."

She shook her head and dipped her chin to her chest. "I'm sorry—"

"Don't apologize." He caught her chin in his fingers and lifted it gently. "Not for going after what you want." He smiled and worked hard to control his breathing. His heart raced, his blood pumping hard with everything *he* wanted. "It's really sexy."

She blushed a little and tried to look away, but he held her chin so she looked directly into his eyes. "It is, Natalie. *You* are."

"I've never been called that before."

Aiden didn't bother trying to hide his surprise. "What? That's insane." It was. It was beyond insane. Natalie was without a doubt the sexiest woman he'd ever laid eyes on. And that kiss? *Damn.* That kiss was fire. If they connected on every level the way they connected with a simple kiss...

With his hand still on her cheek, Aiden stepped closer until he could feel the puff of air of her exhale on his lips. Her tongue darted out again, a trait he was coming to find incredibly sexy...and harder and harder to resist.

And he couldn't resist. He pulled her close, one hand on the flat of her back, the other cupping her face gently, his thumb stroking her soft skin as his lips explored hers. She closed her eyes and sighed as they deepened the kiss.

Where the first kiss was a little tentative and unsure, the second one was nothing of the sort. Her body moved closer to his until her breasts were pressed up against his chest. Electrical shots fired through him, and Aiden worked hard to stay in control despite the fact that his erection was hard and pulsing between his legs. He forced himself to pull away from her—not because he wanted to, but exactly the opposite. If he didn't put distance between the two of them, their relationship might start moving faster than he intended it to. And he needed her to understand that he wasn't looking for that. Well, not *only* that. He wanted more with her. It was still so new, and probably way too early to even think about it, but Aiden couldn't help it. When it came to Natalie, she made him want things he didn't think he'd ever want again.

And he didn't want to screw that up.

As soon as there was a bit of space between them, Aiden swallowed hard and turned back to the espresso machine. "I think I promised you a coffee."

Coffee.

Coffee?

How the hell was she supposed to focus on a coffee when he'd just kissed her like that? And she'd kissed *him* like that?

The memory of how she'd just done it—pushed her nerves aside and gone for it—thrilled her. But not nearly as much as the way her entire body thrilled when his lips touched hers. When he pulled her close and his tongue—

"I think it was a *life-changing* coffee you promised me." She grinned in an effort to act as casually as possible despite the fact that she was feeling anything but. Her body was charged in a major way, as if she could be set off with just one touch.

A full-body shiver ran through her, and Natalie was glad that Aiden wasn't looking at her. Would he be able to tell that she was so completely affected by his kiss? That she could barely stand there without her knees buckling? That formulating words after having her world tilted that way was one of the hardest things she'd ever done? Would he be able to tell that she had absolutely *no* idea what she was doing?

Her first kiss. Her first *real* kiss, because kissing Brandon Ryan when he was such a complete and total douchebag didn't count. She could rewrite her history however she wanted to, she decided. Yes. Aiden had been her first real, adult kiss. And damn, it had been absolutely every single thing she ever could have imagined and so much more.

Was it normal to feel your insides liquify like that?

Was it normal for your toes to curl and feel both nothing and everything all at once?

Natalie had no idea, and she didn't care, because normal or not, it had been amazing. And she wanted to do it again.

But did he?

She watched Aiden, who was intently focused on the elaborate espresso machine. He was prattling on about coffee beans and water temperature and a bunch of other things that didn't seem to make much sense to Natalie, but still, she made an effort to focus.

Was he trying to distract her? Was the kiss no good for him? Did he know that she had zero experience? Had it been terrible?

She needed to get out of her head.

"Don't forget the cups." Natalie moved across the kitchen, fully aware of their proximity once again. She held the cups out.

Aiden turned away from the machine and a smile slipped over his face. They were so close, only the two ceramic cups between them. "Thank you." The words came out gruff and low, and as he took the cups from her hands, he leaned in and pressed one soft, sweet kiss on her lips as if it were the most natural thing in the world for them to be together in the kitchen.

Natalie froze. The feeling of his lips on hers lingered as he once more turned to the machine to make them their life-changing coffees.

But her life had already changed. And it had nothing to do with coffee.

It took another few minutes for Aiden to wrestle the machine into submission and produce two steaming cups of cappuccino. He put them both on a small tray with little spoons and a bowl of sugar—just in case it was too strong—and they moved into the living room.

"I can't even tell you how much I've enjoyed tonight," Aiden said when they were situated on the sectional sofa. They faced each other, which was good for conversation, but not good for kissing, if they were going to do that again. Natalie couldn't help but feel that the seating arrangement was intentional, to keep distance between them. As nervous as she was about their physical relationship and whatever that might look like, the draw to be near him was much stronger than any nerves she had.

"I had a really good time, too." She took a small, tentative sip of her hot coffee. She lifted her head and wiped the froth from her lips with her fingertips before sticking her finger in her mouth to suck it clean.

Across from her, Aiden groaned and shook his head with a laugh.

"What?" Her question was innocent, sure. But also, it was genuine.

"You really have no idea how sexy you are, do you?"

Instinctively, she dipped her head again as she felt the heat from the blush at the back of her ears. Natalie shook her head and when she looked up again, Aiden had put his coffee down and was moving across the space to sit next to her.

"Sorry," he said. "I tried for space, but…do you mind if I sit closer?"

Without hesitation, she shook her head. "Not at all. I was wondering why you were so far away."

"Because I was afraid I wouldn't be able to stop touching you if I sat here." As if to prove his point, his hand came to rest on her thigh. It was a light touch, but it ignited a blaze inside her.

"That's okay." The words came out in a breath. And not for the first time that night, Natalie surprised herself with her boldness. "I don't mind." Her hands trembled so hard, she was afraid she'd spill. With shaking hands, she set her coffee down.

He chuckled a little. "That's a very good thing to hear." He leaned closer. "Because you are proving to be very hard for me to stay away from."

She tried to remember Sarah's of advice to just go with how she felt and not overthink it, but that was proving to be so much easier said than actually done. Because if she just went with how she felt, Natalie was absolutely sure she'd make a huge fool of herself and Aiden would run screaming in the other direction.

But would he?

Too many things flooded through her mind all at once.

Aiden wasn't a stupid high school kid with an agenda to make himself look good in front of his friends. He was a grown man. A grown man, whom, if he was to be believed, found her incredibly sexy. And why shouldn't she believe him?

His lips brushed hers, and the promise of another kiss that would light her body on fire zinged through her. In less than an hour, she'd gone from her first kiss, to her second, to an intense need to want to do a whole lot more than kissing.

But moments before his lips could connect with the promise of so much more, Natalie pulled away. In fact, she pulled away so abruptly, she bounced a little on the sofa. A move that surprised even her.

Natalie laughed, smiled, and tried to swallow her nerves. She both regretted and was relieved with the distance between them.

"Nat? Did I do something wrong?"

The question on Aiden's face, and his immediate concern, hit her in the chest. *No!* she wanted to yell. *You did nothing wrong. Not at all. It's all me!*

Oh. My. God.

Not even a little.

Natalie's mind worked overtime. She was going to screw it all up, just because she was scared and inexperienced. And if that happened, she would never forgive herself.

She swallowed hard and instead of telling him the truth, she simply said, "No." Her voice was weak, and she didn't even recognize it as her own. She was not weak. She was not a scared and timid person.

Everything was all mixed up.

"It's just..." She ran a hand through her hair. She could tell him the truth right now and it would be okay. Wouldn't it? Surely Aiden wasn't the type of man to think less of her because of her past experience, or in this case, lack of it? No. He was definitely not that kind of man.

But what if he treated her differently? Precious or fragile?

Ugh. She couldn't stand it. She wanted her first time to be natural and full of passion. The last thing she wanted was for him to treat her differently because of it. That would be the worst.

"It's late," she said lamely. "And I had such a nice time with you that I think it's best to end it right here, don't you?"

To her surprise and joy, Aiden pressed his lips together with a little laugh and nodded. "I do." He stood and rubbed his hands down the front of his pants. "Because I'm afraid if you stayed, I would have a very hard time sticking to my rules."

"Rules?"

He shrugged a little, suddenly bashful. "I know it's very old-fashioned, but I have rules about dating and...well, sex."

Natalie perked up.

"I don't have sex on the first date." He looked both apologetic and disappointed. "I just think..."

"You don't need to explain. I completely agree."

"You do?"

"Don't look so surprised." She laughed.

"Oh no." He held up his hands. "That's not what I meant at all. I was just—"

"Really." Natalie stood. "It's fine. I really do agree with you."

"I'm so glad." His shoulders sagged with relief. "Because I really like you, Natalie, and, I know it's still early, but maybe things with us could actually…"

He didn't need to finish the sentence. She nodded. "Maybe they can." She gathered up her coat and purse.

"Let me walk you home."

"No. It's fine. I think maybe the space is a good idea."

"I can't disagree." Aiden put his hand on her arm and squeezed gently, as if he were reluctant to let go, as he leaned in to give her a sweet kiss on the cheek. "I really had a great night, Natalie. Can we do it again soon?"

"I'd really like that."

As Natalie turned to the door to leave, she caught a glimpse of the mostly untouched *life-changing* coffee on the table and smiled to herself. She had a very strong feeling that it wasn't going to be the coffee that was life changing but the man who had made it.

Chapter Nine

IT HAD BEEN ALMOST a week since Aiden had almost broken his self-imposed dating rule. A rule that, ever since he upheld it, he'd been regretting. Everything had felt so right with Natalie. The date had gone perfectly. They were connecting. And the kiss. *Damn, that kiss.* If that kiss, and the one after it and the one after that, was any indication of the chemistry that they had together, they were going to absolutely explode when they finally came together.

Whenever that would be.

Aiden was starting to feel like a second date might never happen.

He needed to keep reminding himself that it had only been a week and he needed to be patient. Still, it was frustrating that despite multiple attempts, their schedules just hadn't matched up. Maybe it was true that absence made the heart grow fonder, but he was starting to really miss her. Which meant he was going to have to start getting creative about spending time with her. Because even if they couldn't squeeze in an actual date, he really didn't want to go another whole week without seeing her face.

And he could do creative. Especially if it meant sneaking in a quick kiss.

He was also acutely aware that he needed to tell her about Brenna. An honest relationship meant honesty on both sides, and he wanted to be forthcoming with it. Especially before things got more serious, and he *did* want them to get more serious.

But the idea of telling Natalie about his ex didn't thrill him, and he couldn't seem to find a way to bring it up casually. To be fair, he hadn't really had a chance to drop that kind of bomb. And the more he thought about it, the less he wanted to ruin a perfectly good date by talking about his ex, but still. He would.

Soon.

He finished marking the last of the papers he'd assigned to his senior students and pushed them to the side of his desk before packing up and leaving the school behind, excited by his newly formed plan.

After a quick stop to Sweetie Pies, Aiden walked into a very quiet fire station. "Hello?" With the bakery box in hand, he walked through the parked trucks to the back staircase that led to the lounge.

"Hey there." A man jumped up when Aiden approached. "What can I help you with?"

"I'm looking for Natalie." Aiden looked around the lounge, but aside from a few other guys, he didn't see Natalie. "Is she around? I thought she was working today."

"She is," the man answered. "But she's actually out on an inspection right now."

Disappointment coursed through Aiden.

"I'm Jason. Can I help you with anything?"

"Unless you can turn into a cute blonde, I don't think you're going to be much help." Another man joined them. He stuck out his hand to Aiden. "Hi, I'm Jeremy Davis. You must be Aiden."

Aiden chuckled. "I am. But I don't think we've met." Aiden had heard of Jeremy, certainly. Everyone had. He was involved in the hotel fire a few weeks ago. It was Natalie who'd dragged him out to safety, right before she'd delivered Hope's baby. He had no right to it, but a rush of pride flowed through him. Natalie really was amazing.

"We didn't have to." Jeremy shook his head with a smile. "It's a small town, and everyone has a way of knowing everything in Glacier Falls. In a good way," he added quickly.

"Of course a good way."

"And one of the things that I know is that you and Natalie are…dating?"

"Yes." Aiden nodded. "I guess you could say we're dating."

The other man, Jason, made a noise that was a cross between a sigh and a low growl. Aiden turned to look at him, but Jason's face didn't give anything away. "Are those honey buns?" Jason reached out for the box.

"They are," Aiden said. "I brought them for—"

"I'll make sure she gets them." Jason took the box and walked off in the direction of the kitchen.

Aiden was pretty sure Natalie would never see the baking, but it was a fight he wasn't willing to jump into. Besides, he'd personally see to it that Natalie got as many honey buns as she could handle. He shook his head and turned back to Jeremy.

"Don't worry about him," Jeremy said to his unasked question. "I think he has a little crush on Nat. He'll get over it. And I'll make sure she knows you stopped by. It was good to meet you."

"You, too. I've heard a lot about you."

Jeremy laughed. "For better or worse, I guess. Getting knocked out in a fire isn't really the best reputation to have."

"But I also heard you're going to be the new chief. Congratulations."

"Thank you." Jeremy beamed. "There's going to be a bit of a ceremony next weekend and a party afterward. It would be a great time to get to know some more people in town, if you're up for it."

Aiden grinned and answered honestly. "That actually sounds great. Thank you for the invite. I'll be there."

"Great, man." Jeremy slapped him on the back. "We'll see you then." He turned to go. "And don't worry, I *will* tell Nat you stopped by."

"Everything looks great here." Natalie marked another check on her clipboard and the fire inspection form, and slipped her pen into her pocket. "There's absolutely nothing that isn't perfect about Birchwood." She looked up with a smile to Brody Morris.

"Well, I don't know about that." He shook his head seriously. "I think the soup last night was a bit too salty."

They both laughed.

"I doubt that very much," she said. "Everything I've ever eaten here has been absolutely amazing." Every part of that first date with Aiden had been amazing. The food, as delicious as it was, turned out to be a very small part of that particular date. "I actually look forward to trying more soon."

"Well, in that case…" Brody grinned and flipped a towel over his shoulder. "How about a quick bowl of today's soup? I mean, if you're allowed. Are you still working?"

"Technically." She nodded. "But I'm sure I can have a lunch break. It shouldn't be a problem."

Just to be sure, she typed a quick text to Jeremy, who gave her a thumbs-up emoji in return.

A few minutes later, Brody slid a bowl in front of her. "It's a roasted tomato bisque today." He sat across from her.

"It smells delicious." She dipped a spoon in and blew on it for a moment before putting it in her mouth. "Oh my goodness, Brody. It's amazing. It reminds me of a super elevated version of the soup my mom used to make. It's like..." She took another taste. "Both familiar and totally new at the same time."

"Perfect!" He seemed pleased with her assessment. "I'm glad you like it."

"Anytime you need a taster, I—"

They were interrupted as the front door to the restaurant opened and Sarah walked in. Brody immediately jumped up to greet his wife and kiss her on the cheek. "Just in time, babe. Natalie says my soup is the best thing she's ever tasted anywhere."

"Well..." Natalie laughed. "I don't think I actually said that, but it is pretty damn good."

Sarah rolled her eyes, but Natalie could see the love she had for her husband.

"You're just jealous," Brody said.

"Maybe so," Sarah said. "But I can't spoil my dinner. I promised Rory we'd have pancakes."

"Breakfast dinner? And I'm missing it?"

Sarah shrugged. "You have to work. I guess you'll just have to settle for having the best soup in the whole world while we eat pancakes."

"It's a sacrifice, to be sure." He kissed her again. "Why don't you sit and visit while Natalie enjoys her amazing soup and I'll finish up a few things in the back?"

The couple had so much love and adoration for each other, it was inspiring. Natalie smiled to herself as she ate another spoonful of soup. *Maybe one day, she and Aiden might—*

"So?" Sarah said as soon as they were alone. "How did

your date end with Aiden the other night? I need to live vicariously through you."

Natalie almost choked on her soup. "I doubt that's a thing." She raised her eyebrows.

"Okay, okay, I don't need to do that. But I still want to know." She leaned her elbows on the table. "Were you able to keep your nerves in check?" Just as quickly as she asked the question, she shook her head and sat back. "Never mind. You don't have to tell me. I'm just being nosy and—"

"No." Natalie put the spoon down. "You're not being nosy." She laughed at Sarah's expression. "Okay, you *are* being nosy. But it's fine. I appreciate your concern," she said honestly. "And really, I don't have any...well, I've never had any girlfriends who I could confide in like that, so I really do appreciate it."

Sarah's smile was warm and encouraging.

"So...the rest of the date, well...it was really nice. We went back to his place and—" Sarah's eyes widened in shock and Natalie quickly clarified. "It wasn't like that."

Immediately, her friend looked disappointed.

"Well," Natalie said. "It *was* like that, but it wasn't." Quickly, Natalie filled Sarah in on how things had gone down at the end of the date and where they'd left things. When she was done, she once again picked up her spoon and continued eating while Sarah sat back and shook her head.

"I'm impressed," she said after a moment. "Aiden sounds like a true gentleman. But also..."

"What?"

"He really likes you." She wiggled her eyebrows with a smirk.

Natalie didn't doubt that he liked her, not really. But *really* like her? In the way that Sarah was implying? Like, really really like her?

Maybe.

"Why do you think that?"

"Because he didn't try to sleep with you. Obviously."

Natalie laughed. "Obviously."

She had no idea whether that's what it meant or not, but Natalie couldn't help but hope her friend was right. And even though she didn't have a lot of experience with men, she knew enough to know that the way he'd kissed her had definitely meant he liked her. And she liked him, too. A lot.

Which was exactly why she didn't want to screw it up.

"And I bet he was really understanding about—"

"I didn't tell him." Natalie looked down at her soup, stirring it with intensity so she wouldn't have to meet Sarah's gaze.

"You didn't tell him?"

She shook her head.

"But why? I think he'd understand."

"That's the problem." Natalie put down her spoon and looked up at her new friend. "I don't want him to be understanding. I don't want him to treat me any different. And if I tell him that I'm a"—she leaned forward and whispered the word—"virgin..." She squeezed her eyes against the word that only recently had started to bother her. She'd never before been upset with her virgin status, but now with Aiden, things were different. Very different. "You're right," she continued. "If I tell him, he'll be a perfect gentleman and want to take things slowly and...no."

"No?"

Natalie shook her head again. "No. I really like him, and I feel like maybe it could turn into something. I don't want to screw it up."

Sarah tilted her head. She opened her mouth but closed it again without saying anything. "I really don't think that you could screw it up by telling him that, Natalie. But I also think you need to do what you feel is best."

Natalie nodded, satisfied that she'd talked herself into the idea she wasn't fully sold on earlier. "Right," she said to herself. "What's best."

Less than an hour later, Natalie returned to the fire station to finish up her inspection report—if she could stop thinking about Aiden and *what was best* long enough to focus.

"There was a dude here earlier." Jason, one of the guys Natalie liked hanging out with the most at the station, joined her almost as soon as she sat down. He pulled up a chair across from her and sat backward on it.

"A dude?" She looked up. "Did he have a name?"

Jason shrugged. "Didn't catch it."

"Was it Aiden?" There was only one *dude* who Natalie could think of who would just stop by. Her heart raced and there was a tightening low in her belly at the mere thought of Aiden. Yup, if her whole body reacted that way at the mention of his name, she was in trouble. And she was totally okay with it.

"Aiden?" Jason scoffed and pulled his shoulders back in such a way that Natalie put her pen down and stared open-mouthed at him. "How would I know?"

"Did you ask?"

He stared at her, and Natalie couldn't help but laugh.

"So, that's a no?"

"He brought honey buns."

Honey buns.

"So it was Aiden?"

"Maybe." He shrugged again. "Honey buns were good."

"You ate them? Jason?"

"What? They weren't for everyone?"

"You know they weren't, O'Neil."

Natalie looked up as Jeremy joined them.

"Sorry, Nat." He shrugged. "You know what happens around here with baked goods."

She did. There had been a few occasions where donuts or cinnamon buns had come in and they'd been devoured almost at once, as if the crew had never seen a baked good before in their lives. It was actually pretty remarkable. And Natalie would have found this particular time funny, too, if it hadn't been Aiden who'd brought her honey buns, like the honey buns they'd had in the bakery. Together.

If she hadn't been sitting in front of two of her co-workers, one of whom was her boss, she might have swooned. And Natalie was *not* the swooning type. Not even close. In fact, what even *was* swooning?

So instead of reacting the way she wanted to, Natalie swallowed hard and steeled herself. "And?" She looked at Jason. "Were my honey buns delicious?"

Natalie realized a minute too late what she'd just said and how it sounded. "I mean...I...just..."

Jeremy dropped his head with a shake. "I don't know if I should listen to this. I might have to write up a report."

"No!" Natalie, face flaming red with embarrassment, jumped up.

"I'm kidding, Nat." Jeremy held up a hand. "It's fine. I'm teasing."

She sat down in her seat and glared in Jason's direction before turning her attention back to the report she was trying to finish up.

"Sorry, Nat." Jeremy slapped the table. "Didn't mean to distract you from your work. We'll leave you alone. Right, Jason?"

For a minute, Jason looked as though he wanted to argue with him, but he swallowed and stood. He flipped the chair around and shoved it under the table a little too hard. "Sorry, Nat."

She looked up at him in question.

"Next time, I'll..." He gave her a look that reminded Natalie of a chastised little boy. "Get his name." He shoved the chair again, hard, so it rattled the table and he walked away.

Natalie looked to Jeremy, who shook his head and chuckled. "I'll talk to him," he said. "I think he's just a little..."

"What?"

Jeremy shook his head. "I think he's just a bit jealous, Nat. I probably shouldn't say anything, but I don't think he likes the attention Aiden is giving you. He'll get over it."

Jealous? Jason?

She tried not to let her surprise show on her face, but clearly failed.

"You didn't notice that he might have a crush on you?"

She shook her head. "Not even a little. He does?"

Jeremy shrugged. "I don't know for sure, but..." His gaze crossed the room to where Jason had disappeared to and he nodded. "But I think so. Don't worry," he added quickly. "I don't think it's serious or anything. Like I said, he'll get over it if you're not interested."

Her face heated. She liked Jason; he was a nice guy, but... he was her friend. She hadn't even considered him that way. Of course, up until Aiden, Nat hadn't considered any man that way. She silently cursed herself. She was so bad at the whole dating thing. And she certainly didn't want to make Jason feel bad because she was so completely oblivious.

"Like I said, Natalie, I wouldn't worry about it. He's just..." Jeremy's face changed. "Wait. Has he been...has he crossed the line in any way? Because if he has, I want you to know as the new chief, it's my job to make sure that you feel safe at—"

"No!" She held up her hands. "No," she said again. "It's not like that. Not at all. Jason has been nothing but a friend. It's just that I...don't worry." She smiled as the tension seemed to slip out of Jeremy. "Like I said, I had no idea because I'm completely oblivious to this type of thing." Natalie laughed. "And I just don't think of him like that at all."

"Okay," Jeremy said. "If you're sure then."

"I am. I promise. Jason's a good friend, and he's never been anything but great. Well, except for eating my honey buns." They laughed and the tension of the moment was gone completely.

"Before I forget," Jeremy said. "The wilderness emergency kits you requested are in. And the tools for the first-aid training. I think it's a great idea, by the way."

The warm rush of satisfaction flowed through her. She hadn't been sure how it would be received when she took the idea of wilderness first-aid emergency training to Jeremy, but he'd been supportive right away. And had even offered to get her the supplies.

"In fact, I can't believe we haven't offered anything like it in the past," Jeremy continued. "I mean, consider where we live, right? I think it's excellent that you've decided to get involved with youth and the high school the way you have."

Wait. No.

She hadn't said she would lead anything. Especially if it involved going to the high school regularly. It was just the one class. Aiden's class.

"Oh, Jeremy." Natalie held up her hands to fend off his ideas before they went too far. "I don't know if I was going to—"

"Maybe more of a club than a class?"

"A club?"

Jeremy slapped his hand on the table and stood to leave.

"Yes. This feels like a good plan and absolutely perfect for Glacier Falls. Thank you for heading this up, Nat. It's a really great way to get involved." He closed his eyes for a moment and nodded quickly to himself. "You know, I'm pretty good friends with Katie Banks. She owns the Hub."

"I know her."

"Maybe reach out to them. They could be a really good resource and a good way to get the community involved."

She still didn't know how she'd gotten herself roped into running a group for high school students, but there didn't seem to be an easy way out. At least not one that wouldn't draw unwanted attention to her. So, Natalie nodded. "I'll do that."

"One more thing," Jeremy said before he left. "This weekend. Are you coming?"

She smiled wide. "To your ceremony? Of course. You're the new boss, after all."

"Right." He laughed easily. "It'll be fun and there's going to be a bit of a get together afterward at Ever After."

"The ranch?"

"That's the one. With everything that happened the first time we tried to do this, we thought why not make it a bit more of an *event*." He ran his hand through his hair. "Okay, it was Bella and Stephanie who thought that, but…"

"I can't say that I disagree with them." Natalie smiled. "It's a huge deal. And especially after the fire and missing the ceremony the first time. You deserve it."

"I guess I do." He shrugged, ever humble. "But anyway, you should come. You're not working that night, right?"

"I'm not."

"Great. And bring Aiden, too."

He walked away, but Jeremy's words echoed in her head. *Bring Aiden.*

Were they a couple? Just like that? Did she just invite him

to things like this so naturally? There were so many questions and it all seemed so hard to navigate. At the same time, Natalie couldn't help but smile to herself, because she already knew the answer.

Yes.

Chapter Ten

HAVING a party for Jeremy's swearing-in ceremony was a great idea, and even though Stephanie couldn't take full credit for it, she would happily take credit for getting Faith and Logan on board to host it at Ever After Ranch. And, of course, for contributing financially to the event. After all, Jeremy was Bella's fiancée, and Bella had very quickly become one of her very best friends.

And even though it had all worked out okay, Steph couldn't help but feel a little bit responsible for the fact that Bella and Jeremy had almost broken up because she *may* have projected her own relationship experience onto Bella. Thank goodness, the two of them were stubborn enough to figure out for themselves that just because Stephanie Starz couldn't make a relationship in the spotlight work, it didn't mean that they couldn't.

So, for even the small part that she played in almost keeping them apart, Steph would do whatever she could to celebrate him. And of course, Jeremy deserved the celebration on his own merits easily.

And, Steph couldn't lie…having a party in Glacier Falls gave her another really good excuse to go home to get as many baby cuddles from little Cole that she could manage *and* check on the progress at Lynx Creek, and of course Travis. Not that she was checking up on Travis. Well, not like that.

Steph and Bella had hoped to fly in early before the ceremony, but shooting was delayed by a day due to rain, and it had set everything back a few days. The trip to Glacier Falls was a non-negotiable for Bella, who was doing a really good job in asserting herself with the producers and directors when she needed a bit of time off from the demanding shooting and recording schedule. She'd made her relationship a priority, just as much as her career, and Stephanie was often in awe of how she was balancing it all. But the delay in shooting had meant that instead of coming in on Thursday, they'd arrived Saturday morning, only a few hours before Jeremy's ceremony.

Bella had immediately gone to be with her love, and Steph had done the same.

"I can't stop looking at him." She spoke to Hope, but her eyes never left her nephew's perfectly chubby face. "He's so perfect, Hope."

"I don't think he's gaining enough weight."

Steph tore her gaze away from the baby long enough to give her sister a look. "What are you talking about? He's perfect. What did the doctor say?"

Hope waved away the question. "I don't think he's getting enough milk." She shook her head. "What if I'm not producing enough for him? What if it doesn't have the proper amounts of nutrients and—"

"Are you breastfeeding?" Steph tried to keep her voice neutral. Hope was obviously stressed, a fact Faith had communicated to her more than once as well. She was worried about their sister, and it was easy to see why.

It didn't look like Hope had slept much at all. She had dark circles under her eyes, and her face was drawn. She'd lost a lot of weight since the baby was born. More than she had to lose, as far as Steph was concerned. Hope hadn't gained much weight in her pregnancy, and in only a month since the baby's birth, she was far thinner than she had been before getting pregnant. Her hair was pulled back into a tight ponytail, but Steph suspected she hadn't washed it lately. And breastfeeding? Steph didn't know all the details, but she was pretty sure that the cancer medications she was supposed to start taking after the baby was born wouldn't go well with breastfeeding.

"I thought you were…" Steph tried to tread carefully. "Well, how are your treatments going?"

Hope shook her head. "It's fine."

But it clearly wasn't.

"Hope? What's going on?"

"Nothing. It's fine. I'm just putting off the treatment for a bit is all."

Shock reverberated through Steph at her sister's words. She tried not to tense; with the baby in her arms, she didn't want him to pick up on any stress, but she couldn't hide the look on her face.

"Don't look at me like that." Hope jumped up from her seat at the kitchen table and busied herself at the kitchen sink, rinsing glasses. It was just the two of them with the baby in the kitchen while the others were in the barn across the yard, putting the final preparations on things for the party later. "The timing isn't right," Hope said, her voice almost lost with the running water. "I need to…"

"What?" Steph adjusted the sleeping baby and stood before walking closer to the sink. "What do you need to do that's more important than treating your cancer?" She tried to keep her voice gentle, but what she really wanted to do was shake her sister until she ran, not walked, to her doctor's office and started the treatments that were going to keep her healthy and save her life. "There is literally nothing more important than that, Hope." Her sister turned and Steph could see the unshed tears in her eyes shining. "Nothing," Steph said again. "You need to—"

"I need to look after my baby." She wiped her hands quickly on a towel and moved to take her baby from Steph's arms. "He's hungry. I need to feed him."

The baby was fast asleep and in no way looked hungry to Steph, but she wasn't about to argue with a new mother. She let Hope lift Cole from her arms and waited while she tucked him close to her body and shuffled from the room, leaving Steph to watch after her. The niggling of concern she'd felt earlier exploded into full-blown worry. She needed to find Levi and see what was going on, because surely she wasn't the only one to notice something was off.

Jeremy Davis was definitely considered to be one of Glacier Fall's favorite sons, which was evident by the turnout for the ceremony that would officially make him the fire chief after Ed Walker, who was equally loved in town, retired. Stephanie was still pretty new to Glacier Falls, but just from looking around, it seemed as if everyone in town had made an appearance. The fire hall was standing room only as the chief officially handed over the role to Jeremy and the crowd applauded for both men.

It warmed Stephanie's heart that she now called a town full of so much love home. She could hear Bella, sitting right up front, start cheering for her fiancé, who beamed brighter when he heard her support from the front row.

"This is all pretty incredible, isn't it?" Faith, who stood next to her with Logan, shook her head in wonder. "I can't believe I used to think this town was so lame."

Logan wrapped an arm around her to squeeze her close. "See? Everything about this town, including everyone in it, is far from lame." He kissed her on the side of the head and she giggled, but didn't try to get away.

"I've changed my mind about a lot of things."

Stephanie couldn't help but laugh, but at the same time she was a little jealous. Faith and Logan grew up together, along with most of their friends. Sometimes Steph couldn't help but feel a little left out because she didn't even know she had sisters until a little while ago. Maybe if she had known, she would've grown up in town with the rest of them, too. It was a crazy thought, and one that didn't even make sense because Steph had been adopted and had wonderful parents and a childhood that had been equally wonderful in a small town that, although it wasn't the same as Glacier Falls, was pretty great, too.

And she wouldn't have changed it. Besides, now that she did know about her sisters, she had the best of both worlds. And as soon as the cabins at Lynx Creek were finished up, she'd fly her parents down and show them her new home and why she loved it so much.

"I'm just glad you changed your mind about me." Logan kissed her with a sloppy kiss that finally made Faith squirm out of his arms.

"Boys are so gross."

Steph laughed, brought back to the moment at hand. "Maybe so, but your gross boy is pretty nice, too."

Logan straightened his shoulders and grinned proudly. "Thank you, Steph. You are definitely one of my favorite sisters-in-law."

She shook her head with a chuckle that quickly faded. "What about Hope?"

"I love her, too," Logan said quickly. "She is also one of my—"

"No." Steph cut him off. "Sorry, that's not what I meant." She looked to Faith, who was watching her carefully as well. "I meant, what is going on with Hope?"

Faith and Logan exchanged glances. Faith pressed her lips together and nodded slightly. Just as she'd suspected, she hadn't been imagining things. Something was definitely up with Hope.

"What is it?" Steph asked. "What's going on with her? Is it her—"

"Maybe we should talk about it later," Faith said quickly. She glanced around the busy room. No one was listening to them, but she was probably right. It wasn't the right time to be talking about private family matters. "But..." She made eye contact with Logan again. "We're worried. Yes."

Steph nodded. She wasn't surprised, but it was good to know that at least she wasn't the only one who'd noticed something was up with Hope. "Okay, let's talk before I have to go back. Whatever I can do."

"Definitely." Faith hugged her impulsively, and Steph pulled her in tight.

She loved her sisters fiercely, and would do anything for them. She hadn't known them long, but it was as if a piece of her that she hadn't known had been missing was finally filled and she was whole again. She would protect that feeling with her life, if she needed to.

"But we should get back to the ranch now and help Levi get set up for the party later."

"Let me know if you need anything. I'm going to stop by Lynx Creek on my way."

"How's Travis working out?" Logan asked and Faith, who didn't miss anything, laughed. "What?" Logan looked between them. "Is he not working out? I thought he'd be absolutely perfect for you and—"

"Oh, I think he's totally perfect for her." She wiggled her eyebrows and Steph rolled her eyes.

Logan looked at them in question. "Did I miss something?"

"You totally—"

"No. Nothing."

Both ladies spoke at the same time, but Steph shot her sister a look to shut her up. No doubt she'd fill her husband in later on her opinions about Steph and Travis. And that's all they were—opinions. Nothing more, because Steph hadn't shared any of her feelings about Travis with anyone. Including her sisters. If they'd jumped to conclusions, or read it on her face, it couldn't be helped. But maybe it could be silenced? She looked at Faith, who was trying and failing not to giggle.

On second thought, maybe it couldn't be silenced either.

She let her gaze travel across the room, where it landed on Natalie Collins. "I'll see you two in a bit. I want to go thank Natalie personally for being so great with Hope and Cole."

Faith nodded. "For sure. Every time I see her, I hug her and thank her again. I think she gets embarrassed, but I can't help it."

"I agree."

Steph said good-bye to them and made her way through the crowd to Natalie, who was talking to a man who looked vaguely familiar, but Steph was pretty sure she hadn't met him yet. "Excuse me," she said, interrupting their conversation. "I don't mean to interrupt, but I just wanted to come over and—"

"Stephanie Starz!" The man's mouth fell open a little, but he caught it and smiled with a shake of his head. "I'm sorry," he said. "I don't mean to…it's just I knew you…sorry. I sound like a total star-struck loser, and I promise I'm not. It's just my…I had a friend who used to absolutely adore you and always had magazines with your pictures, and—"

"No, it's fine." She smiled graciously. Stephanie was used to such reactions. "Hi. It's nice to meet you. I'm Stephanie. You can call me Steph." She stuck out her hand, which he took.

"I'm Aiden Adams," he said. "I teach English at the high school."

"And Outdoor Ed, don't forget," Natalie chimed in. "Hi,

Stephanie. I'm Natalie. We haven't officially met. Not in person anyway."

Steph finished shaking Aiden's hand and immediately pulled Natalie into a tight squeeze. "Thank you so much for everything you did for my sister and my nephew." To her surprise, a tear slipped down her cheek.

"You don't have to thank me." Natalie blushed and dropped her head when Steph finally released her to wipe her eye. "I was just doing my job."

"Maybe so." Steph shook her head. "But you're a hero, and you deserve all of our gratitude. Forever," she added with extra emphasis.

Natalie laughed.

They spent a few minutes making small talk and instantly, Steph liked Natalie. And not just because she'd delivered her nephew in an emergency situation, but also because she was genuinely a nice person. Just like everyone else in town.

"It was really nice to finally meet you in person," she said after a few minutes, aware of the time and that she had to get going. "But I really need to run before the party tonight." Steph looked at them in turn. Her eyes didn't miss the way they stood close together, but not too close, as if they were still unsure of the situation. Aiden also seemed like a genuinely nice person, and a gorgeous school teacher, too. The two of them looked like a good match. They sure looked cute together.

"Will I see you both tonight at the party? There will be dancing." She looked at Aiden when she asked and he chuckled.

"I'm not much of a dancer."

Steph brushed her hair over her shoulder. "Sometimes, all it takes is the right partner. Am I right?" She winked at Natalie before she walked away. "See you both later."

Steph couldn't imagine ever getting tired of the drive from town to Lynx Creek. Now that it was the early days of March, the snow had started to melt and trees were even starting to bud. Green grass was trying to pop through, and she'd been told that it wouldn't be long before she could find a few crocuses here and there. It had surprised her to see that Glacier Falls wasn't still completely covered in snow. After all, it was a mountain town. But, as it was quickly explained to her by more than one local, the town sat between two mountain ranges and the valley experienced warmer spring winds and just a general earlier call to spring. The town always seemed to be at least a few weeks ahead weather-wise than people expected.

Steph may not have expected it, but she sure was enjoying it. Just as much as she was enjoying the drive on the twisty roads. When she turned in to the road that would lead her to Lynx Creek, she stopped for a moment just to look at the entrance. It was her vision to have a huge, oversized log entryway to drive under to greet guests. Maybe some giant boulders with "Lynx Creek Cabins" engraved on them. Nothing too flashy. Just something understated that almost blended in with the surroundings to mark the entrance.

She made a mental note to talk to Travis about it.

If she could find Travis.

Twenty minutes later, she was still wandering around the cabins, equally impressed with the work that had been done so quickly, and annoyed that she couldn't find her general contractor anywhere. She'd told him she was coming and not only would she be staying on-site in her cabin, but she was expecting a progress report.

Maybe she should have been clearer that the progress report was expected to be done in person.

Either way, she didn't have the time to waste, so Steph found her cabin, Bankside, which, happily, was almost done.

She'd seen pictures and was impressed with the progress he'd made on it, but seeing it in person was completely different.

The porch had been rebuilt and was now not only solid and safe, but also double the size it once was. They hadn't discussed that, but it was a nice touch. With a big rocker over in the corner, Steph knew the porch was sure to be one of her favorite places to sit and watch the river. So much so that she didn't even want to go inside right away. But the time pressure was in the back of her mind. She had to get to the party.

Soon, she told herself. Very soon she'd be able to spend as much time as she wanted on the porch.

Inside, the cabin had been completely refinished. The logs were sanded and revarnished so they looked almost new. The kitchenette in the corner had been updated with new appliances and a concrete countertop that blended in nicely. Travis had a good eye for making natural materials work well together. She was impressed.

Sadly, she didn't have too long to look around the space and really appreciate all the details. Not that there were a ton of finishing touches—almost none at all. Stephanie would be putting in some time shopping and working with a designer when it came to the finishing, but there was a pile of bedding on the bed and a few dishes in the kitchen—not that she'd be staying long enough to do any cooking. Still, it was nice that Travis had thought of it. Because she hadn't.

It helped lessen her annoyance with the man for not being there to show her around.

Stephanie dropped her overnight bag, and quickly changed into a clean pair of dark jeans and jade-green blouse that she knew made her eyes pop. She paired the outfit with her tall, black boots, perfect for dancing in the barn, and headed out almost reluctantly. The cabin, although small, was so inviting and cozy. It was far from finished and lacked most furniture still, but nevertheless it felt like home in a way that nowhere since her childhood home had ever felt.

By the time she arrived at Ever After Ranch, the party was starting to heat up. The parking area was full, and she could hear the music even before she got out of her car. It seemed as if half the town was there, which she didn't doubt. But even through the crowd, the moment she walked into the party space that was mostly used to host gorgeous weddings, her eyes locked on one person.

Travis Bishop.

What was he doing there? He was supposed to be working on her cabins. Or at the very least, waiting to show her the work he *had* been doing. He was definitely *not* supposed to be spinning some cute brunette around on the dance floor.

A rush of heat flooded her body and her jaw set in a hard line as she watched the couple move easily to the music. The woman she recognized vaguely—she worked behind the counter at Sweetie Pies, but she couldn't recall her name— smiled and giggled as Travis dipped her low before pulling her up and skipping around the floor in a two-step.

"They look pretty good out there, don't they?"

Stephanie spun to see her sister Faith standing next to her, with baby Cole in her arms. The baby, completely oblivious to the party going on around him, was sound asleep. His impossibly long, dark eyelashes fanned out over his chubby cheeks. At once, Stephanie's heart melted, and the tension in her body released a little. But not entirely.

"He's supposed to be working." She turned back to look at the dancing couple.

"Is he?" There was a teasing lilt in her sister's voice that Steph did not miss. "Because there's a party going on."

"Yes," she insisted. "He—"

"And that's why you look like you're about to go all redheaded fiery temper tantrum right now? Because Travis is supposed to be *working*? It wouldn't have anything at all to do with the fact that he's dancing with Jolene."

"No!" She spun to face Faith again, but her sister's smiling face told her she was just trying to wind her up, so Steph swallowed hard and tried to temper her protests. "I am *not* going to go all redheaded fiery temper tantrum, as you put it." She took a deep breath and pulled her shoulders back. "I was just expecting him to be at Lynx Creek when I got there and when he wasn't, well…"

"No need to explain, sis. I get it." Faith winked dramatically and laughed, causing Steph to roll her eyes.

"I am not attracted to Travis."

"I didn't say you were."

"Didn't you?" She could feel herself getting worked up again. She also knew she was lying through her teeth, and her sister knew it.

Faith shook her head in response.

"Because I'm not," Steph continued. "I mean, just because he's got those dark, smoky eyes, and arms that look like they could wrap me up and throw me—"

"Steph. I don't—"

"And sure…" She was on a roll that she couldn't stop, even if she wanted to. Maybe it was because her thoughts and feelings about Travis had just been building, with no opportunity to get them out. Maybe it was that she was lacking sleep, or she was simply caught up in the moment. She didn't know, but once she'd started talking about him, she couldn't seem to stop. Besides, Faith was a safe place. As much as she liked to tease her, she wasn't going to say anything. "He's got that cocky arrogance that's both super annoying and super hot all at the same time and makes you wonder how confident he'd be in—"

"Steph, maybe you—"

"Clearly the man has moves." She waved her hand in his direction. She'd seen the way he moved on the dance floor. *If he moved like that fully clothed, what could he do between the sheets?* Her breath fluttered in her chest, and she turned to point him out to Faith so she could see for herself exactly what she was talking about. "I mean—"

Her hand slammed mid-point into something hard. Before Steph even lifted her eyes to see what she'd hit, she knew. Her face flooded with color, and she was straight up going to die right there in the middle of the Ever After barn.

"I've got moves, huh?"

Shit. Shit. Shit.

With a massive effort, Steph took a breath and channeled her inner actress as she looked into the very same sexy, smoky eyes she'd just been talking about. She was an excellent actress, but even so, it took everything she had not to react to his gaze that was both teasing and challenging at the same time.

"I was just telling Faith that you've obviously been moving quite a bit up at Lynx Creek because it looks great."

Behind her, she heard Faith choke back a laugh. "I should get Cole back to Hope. He's starting to fuss."

Stephanie didn't turn to say good-bye; she kept her eyes focused on Travis, who fortunately had come off the dance floor alone. Damage control would be hard enough without having to monitor what Jolene told everyone as she served pastries and coffee on Monday.

"Well…" Travis spoke slowly. He tucked one hand in the back pocket of his worn jeans as his other hand tousled his hair.

Her stomach flipped as if she were a lovestruck teenager, but Steph worked to maintain her composure.

"You're right."

"I am?"

He nodded and his lips twitched up in a grin. "Oh yes." He reached out and took her hand.

His touch was like fire against her skin that sent a shot directly between her legs and made her stomach flip upside down. But there was no way she could pull away.

"I definitely have moves." And with as much cocky self-assurance as she'd expect from him, he pulled her closer, pressed his hand against the small of her back and, without asking, guided her to the dance floor, where he showed her exactly what kind of moves he had.

Chapter Eleven

"YOU BROUGHT HIM!" Sarah grabbed Natalie's arm and pulled her to the side of the barn so suddenly, Nat didn't even see her new friend. "That must mean things are going well."

Natalie shrugged, but her smile gave her away.

Things with Aiden *were* going well. They hadn't been able to spend much time together in the last few weeks, but they'd texted and talked on the phone every day, and they had been able to sneak in a few little coffee dates and even a quick lunch or two. And it hadn't taken her very long to figure out that absence really *did* make the heart grow fonder. Or, in this case, it made her body react stronger. Because every time they actually *did* see each other, she experienced a physical reaction to his presence. He didn't even have to touch her, and she had full-body tingles.

And when he *did* touch her...well, her body responded hard and fast in ways that she'd never before experienced.

Desire. Need. Want.

There was no doubt in Natalie's mind that although she'd hesitated earlier, the next time they had the opportunity to be alone, there would be no hesitation. None at all.

"I really like him," she admitted to her friend. "We have a lot of fun together."

Sarah wiggled her eyebrows, and Natalie smacked her arm playfully. "Not like that. At least not yet," she added with a little grin.

"I'm so happy for you. Really." Sarah pulled her into an impromptu hug. "So I won't keep you. Go enjoy him." She spun her around and pushed her back into the crowd as abruptly as she'd pulled her out.

Natalie was still laughing when Aiden came up behind her and slid an arm around her waist as if it were the most natural thing in the world. "What's so funny?"

"Just Sarah." She shook her head, dismissing it. "Where have you been?"

He turned so he was facing her. "Your new boss was introducing me to…" He waved a hand around. "Everyone."

"That's a lot of people." She moved closer to him. She still didn't know how close she should get to him. Or what the rules were when it came to kissing him. *Were there any rules?* Surely, there must be. *Were they a couple? When was it official? Did they need to have a conversation about it like in high school? Or did it just happen?* It was all so confusing.

"Whoa." Aiden pulled away a little and assessed her. "What is going on in your head? I feel like you're a million miles away."

She tried to smile. "I was just thinking."

"It looks like you're thinking about something pretty hard." He moved closer again, this time sliding both arms around her waist to pull her tight to him.

So much for rules.

"Maybe you need a little distraction from whatever it is that has your mind all twisted up?"

"A distraction?" Natalie tipped her head up in question.

Aiden answered with a kiss.

Right there in front of everyone. And it wasn't just a *hello* kind of kiss. It was a *I can't wait to get you alone* kiss. And Natalie had absolutely no problem reciprocating it.

It didn't take her long to forget that they were in a room full of people, most of whom she'd just met. As soon as Aiden slipped a hand up her back to twine his fingers through her hair, she was completely lost to the moment.

Oh, who was she kidding. She was lost the moment his lips touched hers.

Aiden held some sort of magical spell over her. One she had absolutely no interest in breaking. Not if it meant making her entire body come alive the way he did.

Absolutely not.

But then it was over. Aiden pulled away a little and touched his finger to her lips. "I've been wanting to do that since…well, since the moment I saw you today. I didn't think the fire hall in front of your boss on his big day was necessarily the right place, though, so I waited."

It took her a moment to catch her breath, but when she did, she smiled and cupped her hand on his cheek. "It was definitely worth the wait."

"I'm pretty sure that's not going to be the only thing worth the wait."

Her body flared with need, and there was an unmistakable heat between her legs. *Oh, it would definitely be worth the wait.*

If they were at any other function besides the celebration for her new boss, Natalie would have taken Aiden and immediately left with him so that there would be no more waiting at all. But, despite the endorphins crashing through her, trying to convince her otherwise, she sighed and forced herself to take a step back from him. "But I guess we're going to have to wait a little bit longer, because we only just got here."

She surprised herself with her boldness, but at the same time, it felt natural. It wasn't bold. It was the next step and one she wanted to leap into. What was the point in tiptoeing around it? She wanted him.

He nodded his agreement but before he released her completely, he pulled her in for one more quick kiss and whispered in her ear. "All I will be thinking about all night is getting you naked and kissing every inch of your body." He pressed a small, but impactful kiss on her neck and finally stepped away, leaving her with the only thing she'd be able to think about all night, too.

The party was both an extreme form of exquisite torture for Aiden with Natalie looking so damn sexy in her dress that hugged all her curves, knowing that in only a few short hours he'd be taking that dress off her, and also at the same time, a huge amount of fun. It turned out that Natalie was a great dancer. Paired with his moves gleaned from chaperoning more than his fair share of high school dances, they had a great time on the dance floor.

It didn't hurt that anytime he was able to spin her close enough, he gave her a sneaky little kiss.

Aiden couldn't remember the last time he'd had so much fun flirting and building the anticipation of what was going to come next with a woman. And *damn*, what was coming next… he couldn't even let himself think about it if he was going to get through the rest of the party without pulling her into the bathroom to get completely inappropriate with her.

It wasn't a bad idea. But it wasn't the way he wanted their first time together to be.

He planned to take his time with her. Kiss every inch of her, make her squirm with pleasure over and over before finally…

Dammit. He needed to stop thinking about it.

Aiden forced himself to look away from where Natalie was chatting with a few friends. She'd gone to the restroom and been caught up by the women on her way back. He had to fight the urge to go to her. He'd never felt such an urge to be close to someone as he had with Natalie. But he didn't want to come on too strong, despite the feelings he was having that were exactly that. Besides, it would do them some good to spend a few minutes apart. They could use the cooling off time.

He scanned the room and his eyes landed on Damon Banks, who was talking with a man he'd never met and was holding a...baby?

This town, and the people in it, never failed to surprise him.

With a shake of his head, he grabbed a bottle of water from a nearby tub and joined the men. "Hi." He turned to the man he didn't know. "Sorry to interrupt. I'm Aiden Adams. I'm pretty new to town and I don't think we've met."

The other man extended his hand. "Nick Newton" His smile was friendly, if not a bit tired. He pushed his glasses up his nose and added, "This is my daughter Amelia."

The baby was cute, maybe about five or six months old, not that Aiden had any experience with babies at all, and wide awake, busying herself with trying to grab Damon's nose, something both the baby *and* Damon found equally entertaining.

"We've actually just officially moved to Glacier Falls," Nick said. "So technically we're new, too. Nice to meet you."

"Looks good on you," Aiden said to Damon, who had started to make cooing baby noises to little Amelia.

Nick burst out laughing.

"What?" Damon pretended to look offended. "I make this look *good*."

Aiden chuckled as Damon hammered it up, bouncing the baby and making her laugh.

"Let me tell you a secret," Nick said to Aiden. "It turns out that having a cute baby in your arms *does* look good to women. The irony of it is that you're so bloody tired all the time that you don't even have the energy to look at a good-looking woman, let alone ask her out."

Damon tilted his head into the conversation. "Except for one, right?"

Aiden glanced around. "Amelia's mother?"

Nick almost choked on his laughter. "Hardly." He shook his head and reached his arms out for the baby. "It's complicated, man. To say the least. But the one thing that is not even remotely complicated is how I feel about this little peanut." He kissed her forehead and looked back to the men. "I'm going to say a few good-byes and get her home. Good to meet you, Aiden. I'm sure we'll see you around."

He waved and, together, Damon and Aiden watched him cross the room. "He's a good guy," Damon said, almost to himself. "He deserves to be happy."

"It looks like his little girl makes him pretty happy."

Damon nodded and smiled. "She does. But…"

Aiden followed his gaze to where Nick had stopped to talk to a woman who Natalie had pointed out was Jeremy's sister, Charlotte. "Ah," he said. "I see. So you think she can make your friend happy?"

As if he'd been caught out, Damon quickly shook his head and turned his back to the room. "You know what? It's none of my business. I just want my friends to be happy and however they make that happen is up to them." He smiled, showing off a dazzling set of white teeth. "And what about you? How's that class of yours? Is it making you happy?"

Aiden could certainly think of one thing, or more specifically, one woman, who was making him *very* happy and hopefully very soon would make them both even happier. But he was pretty sure it wasn't appropriate to discuss the details of it all with Damon, when they hardly knew each other.

"The class is good." He nodded, moving on to safer subject matters. "Honestly, it's been better than I expected it to be considering I really don't know anything about the area. The kids all have some good ideas about what they'd like to do for excursions for the rest of the year. I guess it's easier when they've all grown up out here in the mountains. Hell, they can probably teach me a thing or two."

"There's no doubt about that." Damon crossed his arms. "Speaking from experience, I can tell you that most of those kids will be able to show you all the best spots. But that doesn't mean you can't teach them a few things, too. And I think Katie and I can help you out with that, if you like?"

They'd casually mentioned helping before, but there hadn't been a real opportunity to talk details. "I'd really like that. More than you know."

Damon laughed. "Together, Katie and I have a ton of experience and...well, I'd really like the opportunity to donate some equipment to your program."

Aiden shook his head. He hadn't heard right. "Donate?"

"I know you were prepared to rent everything," Damon continued. "But if your program has the need for it, I'd be more than happy to donate some equipment. Maybe some packs and tents for overnight treks this spring. And next winter, we can talk about snowshoes or cross-country ski gear."

"Are you serious right now?" As a public school teacher, Aiden was always fighting for access to more funds for his classes and programs. It was an unspoken, built-in part of the job. He hadn't even scratched the surface as to how he was going to run an expensive Outdoor Ed program with no extra funds. Not without massive fundraisers. *But a donation...* He didn't even have the words.

His shock must have registered all over his face because Damon chuckled and slapped his back. "I know it's all coming out of left field. Why don't we talk about it properly next week? We'll have a meeting and lay out all the details, okay?"

"I don't even know what to say, Damon." He shook his head, but slowly the grin slipped over his face. "This is going to make such a difference. Thank you."

"Don't mention it."

Damon excused himself and left Aiden alone.

This day was getting better and better. His eyes scanned the room until they found Natalie. She was laughing at something someone had said. But as if she'd sensed him watching her, she turned, the smile still on her face. Aiden could see her eyes sparkle, even from the distance they were at. She winked.

Oh yes.

As good as the day had been, it was just about to get even better.

Chapter Twelve

THIS TIME when Aiden unlocked his door and let her into his house, Natalie wasn't feeling any of the nerves she'd had before. There was nothing now but excitement.

Not true.

There was also a whole lot of *need*.

It wasn't a sensation that Natalie was really familiar with. Not like this. Sure, there'd been times in the past where she'd been turned on before and had urges. She wasn't a robot, after all.

But this…this feeling that Aiden gave her just by *looking* at her like he wanted to eat her up—*that* was new.

The way her body vibrated with a simple touch from him.

The way she was sure her knees would give out on her.

The way the heat built between her legs until she was sure she would burst open.

All. New.

As was the surge of confidence she was suddenly feeling as she walked into Aiden's living room and shrugged out of her coat. "So," she said as casually as she could. "How about another shot at that life-changing coffee you—"

She couldn't even finish the sentence before Aiden's arm was around her waist. He spun her and pulled her close to him. With one hand at the back of her head, fingers twined through her hair, and the other on her hip, holding her firm, he kissed her. Hard.

A small moan slipped from her mouth as the kiss deepened.

"Coffee." He panted the word against her lips. "Can. Wait."

He kissed her again, nipping at her lower lip as his hand slid down her body so he held her firmly by the hips.

Yes. This passion. This urgency. *This* was why she hadn't told him she was a virgin. It would have changed everything.

The thought slipped through her consciousness, and then just as quickly faded away. All of her focus was on Aiden and the way his hands were gripping her ass as he once again kissed her.

His mouth pulled away from hers and moved to the sensitive skin on her neck and behind her ear.

Natalie had never been kissed like that before. Never had anyone's lips been on her neck before and Aiden's were oh, so good. He nipped and sucked, just a little, and a flood of moisture rushed between her legs.

She squirmed at the sensation he caused in her. And the need that was building to the point of no return.

Not that she planned to stop what was happening. No. Way.

Her hands clutched at Aiden's back as his mouth moved farther down her body, tracing the neckline of her dress, until he abruptly jerked backward away from her.

"Aiden?" Fear flashed through her. *Had she done something wrong? Did he figure out that she was a virgin? Like a big pink sticker on her forehead—was it that obvious?* "What's—"

"I need to see you." His eyes smoldered, dark with passion, and his chest rose and fell in deep breaths. "Turn around."

Confused, she turned around, and a second later, her confusion dissolved, as his fingers found the zipper of her dress and slowly, tooth by tooth, pulled it down. His bare hands moved over her shoulders and slipped under the fabric, slowly pulling the dress down as he went. With the material off her arms, his hands then moved to her waist, where he resumed his tantalizing slow undressing until the dress fell off her hips completely, leaving her standing in only her bra and panties.

Natalie turned. Emboldened by the way he watched her, she reached up behind her to the clasp of her bra. His eyes never left her as the lacy bra fell to the floor and left her exposed.

He sucked in a sharp breath. "Damn, Nat. You are the most gorgeous woman I've ever seen."

The fact that he'd seen other women registered somewhere, but she pushed the thought away. Of course he'd seen other women. It didn't matter. Because he was there with her now. She was the *only* woman.

Aiden kissed her again. And this time his hands moved on her bare skin, igniting a fire in their wake as they moved lower and his fingers teased the edge of her lace panties.

She tensed briefly, but as his fingers slipped down farther between her legs, she naturally found herself opening a little.

"You are so wet, Nat." He murmured in her ear and slipped a finger inside her.

She gasped at the unfamiliar sensation, but her body adapted immediately. And when he slowly started moving inside her, the sensation built quickly.

"Oh my…"

"Yes," he moaned. "Let yourself go."

He kissed her again at the exact moment that the colors exploded behind her closed eyes and she felt as if she were both flying and falling at the same time. Natalie pulled back from him, needing to catch her breath. Her head fell back and still the sensations crashed through her body.

At some point, Aiden moved and once again both of his hands rested on the curve of her hips, his fingers splayed out over her backside. Her eyelids fluttered open to see him watching her intently. His lips twitched up in a small smile and he shook his head a little. "Holy shit, Natalie."

Her body tensed. There was so much she didn't know. *Had she done it wrong?* Surely she hadn't. Because nothing that felt like that could possibly be wrong. Before she could say anything, Aiden's fingers locked around her hips and he lifted her. Instinctively, her legs wrapped around his body.

His own need pressed hard into her and he kissed her roughly. "I need you so bad."

She trembled in his arms but for all the right reasons as he carried her down the hall and into the bedroom—because she needed him just as badly.

Being with Natalie was like nothing Aiden had ever experienced before. And although he didn't consider himself to be promiscuous, he had definitely had his share of sexual partners, particularly when he was younger and dumber and didn't realize how much more amazing the whole thing could be with someone special.

Hell, he was only *just* realizing that now, in this moment with Natalie in his arms.

Aiden knew how special she was when he met her, but he had no idea what that would really mean.

He forced himself not to get too carried away. He wanted his time with her to last. But when she wiggled like that...*damn.*

Once in the bedroom, with her still in his arms and wrapped around him, he carefully lowered her down until she was lying on the bed, almost completely naked with nothing but a scrap of pink lace panties on. Some now, very wet panties. He allowed the sense of satisfaction to fill him.

Oh, hell yes.

He had done that. And he planned to do it again. And again.

And really, as many times as he possibly could, because having Natalie come apart around his fingers had been fucking incredible.

He leaned over her, caging her in with his arms before kissing her again. Her lips were so sweet.

Would she taste that sweet everywhere?

Without a doubt.

Aiden moved down her body, ready to find out, but she stopped him with a hand.

He looked up.

"You are wearing far too many clothes, Aiden. Take them off." The desire flared in her eyes and he was more than happy to oblige.

When he stood in front of her, she propped herself up on her elbows, her body unabashedly on display for him. His fingers shook, not from nerves but from impatience as he pulled his shirt up and over his head, ignoring the buttons completely. His jeans came next. He stripped them and his underwear down in one move. Then he froze.

The way she looked at him completely stopped him. It was a look of wonder and need, and it completely matched how he was feeling about her.

Before returning to the bed, and the woman he was very quickly falling for, Aiden took a condom from the bedside drawer, tore open the package and slid it into place. He was rock hard and despite his desire to take his time, he didn't know how much longer he could stand it before being inside her.

While his back was turned, Natalie had slipped off her panties and the sight of her completely naked to him—for him —was almost his undoing. He rejoined her on the bed and immediately her hands were all over him, exploring and touching. When her fingers reached his throbbing cock, she hesitated. Almost as if she were unsure.

"You're killing me, Nat."

She giggled and wrapped her hand around his length.

"Okay," he groaned. "*Now* you're killing me."

She stroked him once. Twice. And it was almost too much. With a growl, Aiden flipped her to her back again. "Woman, if you keep doing that…"

"What?"

"I won't be able to stop myself."

Her blue eyes flashed and her nostrils flared. "So, don't."

It was the only invitation he needed.

He used his knee to split her legs farther apart so he could nestle his body between them. Beneath him, her breath was coming in fast, shallow breaths. One hand slipped between her legs again, where he found her wet and oh so ready for him. He teased her sensitive bud, making her squirm beneath him.

Aiden kissed her again as he ran his hands up her body until he could capture her hands in his. He pulled her arms up over her head and looked in her eyes as he lifted his hips just enough to press his cock at her entrance. Teasing both of them.

Her breasts heaved and fell with each breath she took.

"Natalie, you are so incredibly sexy."

She sighed as he pressed into her a little more and then, unable to hold off any longer, with one hard thrust, he filled her completely.

Natalie sucked in a sharp breath and her eyes widened.

He stilled, giving her body a moment to adjust. She was so tight around his length.

Her breath came faster, in small hitches. With her hands still held fast over her head, her breasts jiggled with the movement of her breath. Her eyes held his, her lips parted in a small O as he started moving slowly inside her.

"Oh…Aiden…I…"

He paused and released her hands. They moved quickly to his back, sliding down his body until her fingers dug into his ass, urging him on. "Don't stop."

So he didn't.

She moaned as he started to move faster. Harder.

He swallowed the sound with a deep kiss, but only for a moment. He wanted to hear all her sounds as he brought her once more to climax.

He pulled back, moving his hips so he slid almost completely out before thrusting hard inside her again. And again. Harder every time.

So much for taking it slow.

Every time he entered her, she moaned harder, and soon he felt her legs quake beneath his, her climax imminent.

Good. Because so was his.

With one hand, he tangled his fingers in her hair and took her hard and fast as she cried out her pleasure. He felt her come undone around him, her muscles squeezing and clenching until he, too, couldn't hold off. His own orgasm exploded through him.

Aiden collapsed on the bed next to Natalie, but still, unable to resist her, he reached out and pulled her close to him, gathering her up in his arms until he was spooned around her. Her blonde hair spilled out onto the pillow, and he used one hand to smooth it while he nuzzled into her neck, leaving kisses behind. Before too long, her breathing began to slow and she wiggled back into him.

"That was…" She turned her head around so she could see him.

"Incredible?" He finished for her.

She nodded and bit her lower lip before looking away.

It *was* incredible. To put it mildly.

Never in his life had he experienced sex like that. Not even close. There was something different. Something he couldn't put his finger on. But whatever it was, Aiden knew it had everything to do with her. With Natalie and how he felt about her.

It hadn't been long, but there was no mistaking what was going on.

He was falling in love with Natalie.

Hard and fast. But unmistakably so.

Chapter Thirteen

EVERY MUSCLE in Natalie's body ached.

Muscles she didn't even know she had.

It was still dark out, but Natalie guessed it was early morning. Only a few hours after they'd finally fallen asleep. The night before, they'd each drifted in and out of slumber more than once, but every time they woke and started touching and kissing, they'd inevitably end up making love again.

Making love.

That's what it felt like.

Not that she had anything else to compare it to, but being with Aiden had been more than sex. Way more. There was *no* way sex usually felt that good because if it did, why the hell hadn't she been doing that before?

She knew the answer.

It wouldn't have been the same with anyone else.

Natalie shifted in the bed slightly, careful not to wake Aiden. Her entire body was buzzing. Every nerve ending extra sensitive. And there was an ache between her legs that bordered on pain. A good kind of pain because nothing but pleasure had caused it.

There'd been a moment when it had hurt. A few moments, really. But then…it was nothing but amazing.

She slipped from the bed and padded down the hall to the bathroom.

Yes. Everything definitely hurt a little. She finished up in the bathroom and splashed some water on her face. As Natalie lifted her arms up and over her head in a stretch, she caught a glimpse of herself in the mirror. She wasn't naive enough to think that she'd look different afterward. It's not as though she were fifteen, expecting magical things to happen the moment she lost her virginity.

Not at all.

Still. She leaned in and examined herself closer.

She *did* look different.

But only because the smile on her face was so broad and so genuine, she'd never be able to wipe it off. Not that she wanted to.

She wrapped her arms around her body in a quick hug and debated going to the kitchen to figure out the life-changing coffee machine, or crawling back into bed for more snuggles with the man she was very quickly falling for.

Natalie swallowed back a giggle.

What was even happening to her?

Was this what love felt like? Or was it just what it felt like after sex every time?

She had the ridiculous urge to find her cell phone and text Sarah to ask. But no. She didn't want to bring anything or anyone into this moment with them.

Natalie popped her head back into the bedroom. Aiden was still sleeping, so she grabbed his shirt off the floor and pulled it over her head before heading into the kitchen.

Coffee it was.

Besides, she *still* hadn't tried the life-changing coffee. Not that she needed it. Her life had been completely changed already.

Again, she smiled and a little giggle escaped her lips.

She couldn't help it. She just felt so damn good.

Her smile quickly turned to a frown in the kitchen, confronted with the fancy espresso machine.

There were dials and spouts and buttons. And none of them seemed to make any sense at all. Surely one of them had to create the magical coffee.

Natalie spent the next few minutes pushing things and pulling on levers until miraculously hot water started to flow out a spout.

But not hot coffee water.

She laughed and was about to double down on her efforts when the ringing of a phone from the living room caught her attention. Not wanting to wake Aiden—at least not until she could deliver a hot steaming cup of coffee to him in bed, where maybe she could join him—she sprinted into the living room to find the phone and silence it.

Natalie arrived as the caller went to voicemail on Aiden's phone. Still, she picked it up to flip the switch that would silence the phone.

Ten missed calls?

That was a lot of calls.

Brenna Adams.

All the calls had been from a *Brenna Adams*. Aiden's sister? No.

He'd told her that he was an only child. And she already knew that his mother's name was Sherry. Maybe an aunt or cousin? Whomever it was, they really wanted to get hold of Aiden. Natalie hoped it wasn't an emergency. But if it was… Aiden needed to know. *Should she wake him?*

Her thoughts darted to the naked and very sexy man she'd

left asleep in the other room and how she'd hoped she'd be waking him up.

But if it was—

Before she could finish the thought, the phone rang again.

Brenna Adams.

The name and picture of a very pretty dark-haired woman filled the screen.

Without thinking, Natalie pushed the button to accept the call. It probably wasn't her place to answer Aiden's cell phone, but if it were an emergency, it probably shouldn't go to voice-mail again.

"Aiden's phone."

"Who the hell is this?"

Taken aback by the vitriol in the woman's voice, Natalie's good mood faded a bit. "I'm sorry," she said with a shake of her head. "Is there an emergency? Should I get Aiden to—"

"I'd say there's a fucking emergency," the woman's voice snapped on the line.

Natalie's stomach sank. "Oh no." She started to move toward the hallway and the bedroom to wake Aiden, but she froze when the woman spoke again.

"Some random bitch is answering my husband's phone."

Husband.

Surely she hadn't heard the woman right.

Brenna *Adams.*

No. That didn't make any sense. *Aiden wasn't...*

"I'm sorry," Natalie said softly. "Who are you calling?"

"My *husband,*" the woman spat. "Aiden Adams."

Just like that, the floor beneath Natalie's feet vanished and she was somehow floating in the air, above her body. *Husband? Aiden?* It didn't make any sense.

She couldn't feel her legs. Couldn't feel her hands. Nothing. *Was her body even still there?*

Somehow she managed to lower herself to the floor before she fell over, the phone still in her hand, pressed to her ear.

"You weren't expecting that, were you?" Brenna cackled on the other end of the phone.

Was it funny? It wasn't funny. Then why was she laughing?

Nothing made sense and her brain couldn't keep up with her thoughts.

Her mind raced, but at the same time, everything slowed.

"I'm sorry...." She couldn't finish the thought. Why did she keep apologizing to this woman when she should be screaming at her? Demanding answers from this woman who said she was Aiden's *wife*?

Then again, what right did Natalie have to get mad at *her*?

Her stomach roiled and she thought she was going to be sick right there on the floor.

Aiden was married.

And she'd just slept with him.

Worse—she'd just given her virginity to a married man.

Oh God.

She let the phone slip from her hand to the floor. She only vaguely registered Brenna's voice, still demanding to know who she was and why she was answering her *husband's* phone.

Oh God.

Somehow, Natalie found the strength to reach out and push the button that would disconnect the call. She had to get out of there. She needed to get as far away from Aiden and her terrible mistake as quickly as she possibly could.

But first, she just needed a minute.

Natalie squeezed her eyes shut and inhaled, forcing sensation back to her limbs. Just when she thought she had enough strength to stand, Aiden's voice crashed through her, piercing her heart.

"Nat?"

She looked up to see Aiden, shirtless. His lips—the same

lips she'd just been kissing—turned down into a worried frown. "Who was that on the phone?"

When Aiden finally woke, he instinctively rolled over to pull Natalie close to him. It had only been a few hours since he'd last had her in his arms and it was already too long. He had no idea how he was going to function when he had to spend an entire day away from her. She'd worked her way directly to the core of him in such a short time, it should scare the hell out of him. But it didn't. Quite the opposite.

Natalie felt right.

Everything about her felt absolutely perfect. And then when they'd made love...*damn.*

Never before had sex been like that.

Not. Even. Close.

Everything was different with Natalie, in all the best ways. And he wanted it all.

Especially having her sexy, naked body pressed up against his right now.

Except that when he stretched out his arm, the only thing he felt was the bed sheet. Aiden lifted his head.

Her side of the bed was empty.

A flash of disappointment rushed through him. But she couldn't have gone far. She was probably just hungry. After all, they had more than worked up an appetite the night before.

His dick sprung to life at the memory.

"Mmm." He allowed himself a moment to relish in the afterglow of a night full of lovemaking, but the sound of Natalie's voice in the other room caught his attention.

Who was she talking to?

Aiden reluctantly left his bed, found a pair of sweatpants in his closet, and tugged them on. He hoped he would be taking them off again very soon. Correction. He hoped *Natalie* would be taking them off again.

He heard her voice again. She was obviously on the phone, and although he didn't want to intrude, it was early still. *Who could be calling her so early? And why did she sound...upset? Different.*

When Aiden walked down the hall to the living room and saw her crumpled on the floor, her bare legs tucked up under her, he froze for a moment.

"Nat?"

She looked up and that's when he knew something was wrong. *Very* wrong. "Who was on the phone?"

Natalie didn't answer right away. Instead, she wrapped her arms around her knees and hugged them close. Her eyes moved over the floor to where the phone—his phone—lay.

"Is that *my* phone?" He looked from his cell back to Natalie, who'd turned her head and was watching him. He couldn't read the expression in her eyes. But it wasn't good. Not good at all. "Natalie? Who was on the phone?" he asked again. This time a little sharper than he'd intended.

It was as if his voice had activated something inside her. She sprung up to standing. His shirt looked damn good on her, and Aiden couldn't stop his eyes from going to the hem of the shirt and the creamy bare skin of her thighs. But his gaze returned to hers immediately. Because something was definitely wrong.

Very wrong.

He needed to know. Now.

"Natalie. Were you looking at my phone?"

"What?" She shook her head in disbelief. "Was I *looking* at your...no." She dropped her chin to her chest for a minute and when she looked up again, her eyes shone with tears. "I'm not doing this." She turned to leave into the kitchen.

What the actual...

On the floor where his phone still laid, the screen lit up with Brenna's face.

Fuck.

He'd completely forgotten about Brenna. He'd been so wrapped up in Natalie and getting to know her and being with her that he'd...*shit.* He'd never told Nat about Brenna.

It all made sense. Well, not really. Not completely. But it made some sense. Enough to figure out what had happened.

"Natalie." He reached out and grabbed her arm before she could get away. "I need to...let me—"

She spun on him. Her eyes blazed, the tears gone, and her jaw was set. "Don't touch me." She spoke through clenched teeth. "Don't ever touch me."

He tried to act as if her words hadn't hurt. But they did. They hurt like hell. "Nat, did you answer my phone?" He hated that he could hear the accusation in his own voice. Natalie didn't deserve it. But if what he thought had happened *had* actually happened and she'd spoken to Brenna, there was no telling what she was thinking.

"Yes." She pulled her arm from his grip, but thankfully didn't try to leave again. "I did answer your phone because I thought maybe it was an emergency. The same number kept calling and you were sleeping and..." She dropped her head again. Her shoulders sagged too. "You're married, Aiden? *Married?*"

When she looked up at him, there was so much pain on her face, he felt it acutely in his gut.

"No. I'm—"

"You're not? Brenna's not your wife?" There was a flicker of hope on her face. Of understanding.

But as soon as he spoke again, it vanished.

"No. I mean—"

He didn't have the chance to finish, because in a flash,

she'd moved past him to the hook where she'd hung up her coat.

There was no way she was going to leave wearing only his shirt and…yes. She definitely was.

Natalie had shrugged her coat on over the shirt.

"Nat. Don't go. Not like this. You need to let me explain."

"Do I?" When she looked up, tears streamed down her cheeks. "You're married, Aiden. You have a *wife*. And I…" She shook her head and a noise that was a cross between a laugh and a snort came out of her. "And I'm an idiot because I slept with you and I…ugh, I'm so stupid. I thought you were special and I lost my virginity to you and I thought it was something—"

"Wait. What?" His brain caught on one word. "Virginity? You lost your…you were a…"

"Yes!" She wiped her nose roughly with the back of her arm. "I was a virgin, okay? And I thought you were…oh God. I thought you were different and it was…"

Too many feelings flashed through him all at once. Panic that she would leave. Confusion that she wouldn't hear him out. Hurt that she hadn't trusted him with the secret that she was a virgin. Anger that she'd lied. *A lie by omission.*

But that wasn't fair, was it? He hadn't told her something, too. He hadn't told her about Brenna. That was different. It wasn't a…

Shit. He'd been rough. He'd been—dammit. He never would have taken her so hard had he known she was a virgin.

"Why didn't you tell me, Nat?" He ran a hand through his coarse hair and tugged the ends a little. "I would have taken my time, and been—"

"That's just it!"

She was sobbing uncontrollably and more than anything, Aiden wanted to pull her close to him and erase the last few minutes. To start over, in bed with her, only their naked bodies with nothing between them. Now there was so much between them.

Too much.

"You would have treated me differently," she continued. "And I...it doesn't matter. I made a mistake. You lied to me and—"

"You lied too."

That stopped her.

"What?"

He crossed his arms, more to keep from reaching out to her —the need to touch her so undeniably strong—than anything else. "You lied, too," he said again. "You didn't tell me you were a virgin."

"It's not the same."

It wasn't. It was worse. Or maybe it wasn't. He didn't know. Everything was so jumbled up. He couldn't think straight.

"You're *married*, Aiden!" Her hands fell to her sides and in that moment, with her coat over her bare legs, her hair still tousled from their night of passion and tears streaming down her face, she looked so lost and broken that it caused him physical pain not to touch her. "How could you be married?"

"I'm not married."

"But Brenna—"

"Is my ex-wife." His voice was gentle. "I'm not married, Natalie. I wouldn't do that to you. I would never lie to you."

A lie by omission. He *had* lied. And she *had* lied.

They'd both kept something from the other person. Maybe he didn't know much about relationships, but he *did* know that was the kiss of death. They were just starting out and they were already...it was too much. He couldn't do it again. He couldn't go through that type of relationship again.

And there it was.

This time he'd put a stop to it before it went too far.

They stood in silence for a moment, but finally Aiden shook his head. "Maybe you should just go."

He regretted the words the moment they came out of his mouth. He didn't want her to go. He wanted her to stay. He wanted them to talk about this so they could both explain. But also…

He'd spent too long cleansing himself of one bad relationship to jump back into another one that clearly wasn't what he thought it would be. Maybe Natalie just wasn't the woman he'd thought. And maybe he wasn't ready yet either.

Damn. The idea that he could have been wrong about her, about *them*, hit him in the gut. But there was no way. He couldn't have been so wrong when it felt so…*fuck*.

"Natalie, I—"

"No." She cut him off. "You're right." Again, she wiped her nose roughly with the sleeve of her coat. "I should go. This is…this was…"

Don't say mistake. Don't say mistake. Don't say mistake.

He willed her not to say it. Yes, he was upset. His feelings were twisted and he didn't know where to go from here. Hell, he didn't know *what* he was feeling at that moment. It was so much. So many things. But a mistake? God, no. What they'd done, how it had felt to be with her…

Don't. Say. Mistake.

"This was such a mistake." She sighed and opened the door to leave. "Good-bye, Aiden."

And then she was gone. Her parting words were so much worse than he could have imagined because there had been a finality in the good-bye that hurt more than anything else could have.

Chapter Fourteen

STEPHANIE ONLY HAD one day left before she needed to return to Los Angeles and her shooting schedule. Thankfully, she wasn't the lead in *Bombshell*, or she would have already been back to work. Bella had flown back the morning after Jeremy's ceremony and party, and Steph knew that only three hours after she landed, she was already in hair and makeup to get back on set.

She also knew Bella was having the time of her life. Her new friend was born to be a star and this movie, when it came out, was absolutely going to launch her into superstardom territory. She was so excited for her, that Steph could hardly wait.

She was almost as excited for the movie as she was for Lynx Creek. Okay, she was *way* more excited for her cabin project. Especially after spending the last few days on-site and watching the way it was coming together with her own two eyes. It was *so* much better than looking at it through pictures or video chatting. So much more real to see it all in person and to talk to him face-to-face.

Him.

Thoughts of Travis always pushed their way into her reality. Even when she was purposely trying not to think about him. Which was a lot of the time lately. Because if she didn't actively push him from her mind, he would take over. The way he just had. Again.

His thick, muscular arms. The way he smelled of wood and coffee and peppermint all mixed together in one heady cologne when he'd held her tight on the dance floor. Steph had danced with dozens of men at a variety of functions over the years, but there had been no man who'd made her feel like Travis did when he spun her around the wooden barn floor.

Like she was both floating out of her body and also extremely present in living color at the same time. Like she never wanted him to let go. Like she wanted him to—

"This place is sure coming along, Steph." Nick, with baby Amelia strapped to his chest, sat in the empty rocker on the porch next to her. "I'm impressed with how much you've done in such a short time."

She shook her head and laughed. "I appreciate it, Nick. But I didn't do a thing. This is all the work of Travis Bishop." Just saying his name aloud gave her a thrill. This man was getting to her. Bad.

"Right." He shook his head. "You know, I've never actually met him."

"I'll introduce you." Steph glanced around, but she hadn't seen her contractor all day. She thought maybe he was working on some of the cabins farther up away from where she stayed. She couldn't help but feel that he purposely stayed out of sight when she was around. To give her privacy, probably. At least she hoped that was the reason. Not that he was avoiding her. But why would he be avoiding her?

After all, did a man who was avoiding you keep you on the dance floor all night until your feet finally throbbed so much you begged to sit down? Steph thought back to the party a few days earlier. They'd danced for hours. And laughed and flirted with their eyes…at least, she thought they had. But they hadn't talked. Not really. And despite her wishing he would, he hadn't made a move at all. She was so sure she'd felt a connection with him. But then again, maybe he was just the type of guy who made all women feel as if they were the only woman in the room.

Come to think of it, Travis Bishop was definitely that type of man. The *God's Gift to Women* type of guy.

"Hello?" Nick waved his hand in front of her face. "Earth to Steph. Where did you go there?"

She shook her head and smiled. "Sorry, I don't… It's nothing."

"Right. It would have nothing to do with a certain over-sized hulking cowboy dude who's fixing up your cabins, would it?"

She looked at him in pretend shock. "So you do know him?"

Nick laughed and baby Amelia giggled along with him. "I didn't say I didn't *know* him. I said I'd never *met* him. And it seems maybe I touched on a little something there."

She shot him a look.

"Am I wrong?"

Steph valued her friendship with Nick. A lot. And she couldn't be happier that he'd decided to move his little family to Glacier Falls. But his proximity did come with a few other issues. Like the fact that he was ridiculously observant and, worse, wouldn't hesitate to call her out on her bullshit.

"Why don't we talk about *your* love life?" Without much grace, she changed the subject.

But Nick just laughed. "Nothing to talk about there." He lifted Amelia in the snuggly. "This little one right here is the love of my life."

"I don't doubt that for a minute." Steph tickled under the

baby's chin, making her smile. "But there is other kinds of love."

"Not for this guy." Nick shook his head. "Amelia's all I need. Besides, who has the time? I've been thinking, too, that maybe it's time to think about a project of my own. Like you have Lynx Creek." He tipped his head in consideration. "And I haven't really had anything to focus on business-wise since the microchip with Damon. It could be fun."

"It could be fun. Would you hire some help for Amelia then?" She spoke carefully because it was a sensitive topic for Nick. For reasons that Steph could not even begin to understand, her friend insisted on doing everything and being everything for the little girl ever since she was dropped on his lap—literally. Even after he confessed to her that the baby wasn't likely his blood relation, he'd insisted with a ferocity that he didn't want or need help. It was more than a little concerning for Steph. So if he was willing to hire some help, that was a good sign. For sure.

"Maybe. If the right person comes along."

"Sounds almost the same as dating." She winked, and he only shrugged and looked away. "Wait." She sat up. "Have you met someone?"

"Yes. No." He shook his head. "I don't know. Maybe." He stood to leave. "I should get going."

"Whoa." Steph jumped up after him. "You can't just drop that on me and take off."

Nick laughed as they walked to his SUV. He unstrapped Amelia and handed her to Steph to say good-bye before putting her in her car seat. "It's nothing," Nick said when he was finished buckling in the baby. "I just met her, and I don't really think she's in the space to date anyone yet anyway. It's just—"

"Charlotte Davis." Steph nodded. She'd seen the way they'd hit it off last month after the showcase for *Bombshell*. The woman *had* been through a lot, fleeing a destructive relationship, and Nick was right—she was probably not at all in a position to date anyone yet. But then again, Nick probably wasn't either. The friendship could be good for both of them. "I don't know her very well," she said. "But she seems great."

Nick nodded and tried to look casual. "Like I said. I barely know her either, but being new to town, it might be nice to get to know a few more people."

"Absolutely."

Nick leaned in and gave her a kiss on the cheek, the way he always did.

She squeezed his arms and waved good-bye as he drove away. It was only after he'd driven out of sight that Steph turned and saw the glimpse of movement in the trees by the main building. *Travis?*

She took a step forward and narrowed her eyes, trying to see, but couldn't see anything more than the pines and the smaller leafy trees that were just starting to come back to life after their winter slumber.

Maybe she'd been imagining it. But she didn't think so. And moreover, she hoped she hadn't.

"You're not avoiding me, are you?" Stephanie asked Travis point-blank a half hour later when she went searching for him. If he wasn't going to come to her to give her the update she needed, she'd find him. Either way, she wanted all the information before she left to go back to work.

He turned slowly, a hammer in his hand. "Not at all." His words came slow and heavy, like honey off his tongue.

It sent a chill through her, and she wrapped her arms around herself so she wouldn't shiver under his gaze.

"You were busy."

"I was?"

"With your boyfriend."

Boyfriend?

Stephanie shook her head, but Travis turned around and back to his work without further explanation.

"My boyfriend?" She moved so she was in front of him.

He glanced up at her, but didn't stop his work, pulling nails out of an old board and dropping them into an old coffee can.

"Oh…Nick?"

Travis tipped his head to the side in a slight, sharp gesture. He made a noise that Steph could only describe as a grunt.

Nick? Was he jealous of Nick?

She couldn't help it. A snicker escaped her lips. A hand flew to her mouth as he finally stopped working and looked up at her.

"Something funny?"

Steph couldn't stop the full laugh that burst from her mouth at the same time that she shook her head. "No. Nothing's funny."

Travis dropped the hammer on the pile of boards and crossed his arms over his chest. Despite the chill in the air, he didn't wear a coat. His flannel shirt was rolled up, exposing his strong forearms.

How would it feel to be wrapped in those arms?

The thought popped into her head so quickly, it sent a flush through her body. She quickly shook it off.

"You sure?"

She forced herself to swallow her laughter. "So you *were* watching me earlier, weren't you?"

"You can't answer a question with another question." His eyes sparked and challenged her.

She tipped her head and her long red hair fell over one shoulder. "I don't know if you know this about me, but I can do whatever I want."

It was meant to be flirty, but Travis snorted, shook his head and picked up his hammer again.

"Yeah. I got that about you." He resumed work on the boards.

Something about his dismissive reply sparked her anger. As a redhead, Steph definitely had a fiery temper. It was something she'd worked hard to keep under control when she was younger, especially when she became a celebrity. The last thing she needed was her temper flaring on set or worse, when the paparazzi was watching and could sell a twisted version of the truth. She'd resolved early on not to give them any ammunition, and over time it got easier and easier to keep her temper under control.

But something about Travis Bishop pushed every single one of her buttons, and not all of them were good. She crossed her arms tightly and spread her feet almost to brace herself against the feelings crashing through her as she stared at him. "You don't know anything about me."

He must have heard the change in her voice, because he slowly looked up and examined her. "You don't think so?"

"No." She gritted her teeth.

"I think that I know you and your type better than you think."

Her type?

Rage bubbled just below the surface. Stephanie tried to control it. She tried to push it back down. She couldn't let him get to her. She couldn't let him be the cause for an explosion. It had been so long; she'd done such a good job pushing it down. She took a deep breath the way she'd been taught. In through the nose, out through the mouth.

"You think just because you have money that you can—"

"Stop right there." She held a finger out and was instantly annoyed with herself for how it shook. "Don't say anything that will cause you to lose your job."

He pressed his lips together and took a step back. "Got it, *boss.*"

"Because I don't know who you think you are all of a sudden." Her words were clipped, only barely under control. "But I think it's important that we remember who exactly is writing the check."

What was she saying?

She sounded exactly like the type of person she hated. Exactly like the type of person that no doubt Travis had *just* been referring to. She wasn't that person. She was nowhere near that person. *What were these words coming out of her mouth?*

Disgusted with herself, Steph snapped her mouth shut.

"Like I said. Got it." Travis's words were rough, but she'd be dammed if she didn't see his eyes twinkle when he said it.

Was he taking pleasure in getting her riled up? Was he provoking her on *purpose*?

She couldn't stick around to find out.

With a deep breath in, Steph turned to go but before she did, she said one more thing over her shoulder. "And I know you were watching me, so you can drop the act." With a sharp exhale, she moved to walk back to her cabin as quickly as she could. She needed space before she erupted completely.

But a hand on her arm stopped her in her tracks. It was tight, but not dangerously so. But when Travis spun her around so she was only inches from him, close enough that she could smell the mix of wood and coffee and peppermint that was distinctly his, she saw the danger in his eyes. The way his nostrils flared. Unwillingly, she trembled, but he didn't release her.

But he didn't speak, either.

They stared at each other. Their breathing came quickly. Their chests rose and fell almost in time, while something, some kind of electricity, zinged in the air between them.

Was he going to kiss her?

His breath came fast.

Did she want him to?

Yes. No.

Definitely yes.

Desire and anticipation and the slightest little bit of fear mingled together in a heady combination that muddled all her feelings.

Finally, after what felt like hours, Travis, his hand still on her arm, leaned close.

She sucked in a breath and instinctively closed her eyes for the kiss that was sure to come.

Instead, he released her abruptly, leaving her off-balance. She snapped her eyes open to see he'd taken a step back.

He'd removed his cowboy hat and with his other hand was roughing up his hair. "Sorry," he said gruffly. "I shouldn't have done that." He never looked at her, just turned, grabbed his hammer again and walked away.

Disappearing into the pines and leaving Steph to stare after him, wondering what the hell had just happened between them. Because whatever it was, it had left her wanting more.

Chapter Fifteen

IT HAD BEEN three days since everything had blown up and still Natalie couldn't figure out how things had gone so wrong with Aiden. Yes, she'd withheld information from him, but it was *hers* to give. *He* hadn't told her he'd been married before! And that was a *way* bigger deal than her virginity.

She just couldn't understand it. Everything had been going so well and then…

She moved through her days, performing her duties at the station on autopilot, grateful for any emergency callouts because they meant she could escape her thoughts and memories long enough so she didn't have to feel the panic and hurt that had consumed her since leaving Aiden's house. But then the emergency would be resolved and her day would once more grow quiet enough that it would all rush back to her as though it had just happened.

When she'd woken up in his bed, everything had been right. *So* right. She'd never felt such a sense of completeness before. Of full-body happiness. How could something that felt like that be wrong? It wasn't wrong. It was all kinds of perfect.

And then she'd remember. It hit her out of the blue, like a wrecking ball in an old, abandoned building.

The phone ringing.

Smash.

Brenna. His wife.

Smash.

His face when he heard that she'd kept a secret from him.

Smash.

And that was it. The way he'd looked at her, as if he didn't trust her. Like he didn't trust himself. It was as though he were giving up. But she hadn't done anything wrong. Had she?

No.

It didn't matter how many times she went around it in her head. Not telling Aiden that she was a virgin wasn't an offense that should destroy a relationship. It was *her* secret. It wasn't anyone else's business. Not like having a wife. *That* should have been her business.

She dropped her head to the table. Everything was so messed up. She hadn't felt so terrible since…

Since high school.

It took her a few days to realize it: The awful, all-encompassing body ache; the numbness in her feet and hands. The dizzy sensation when she thought about Aiden. The way her stomach couldn't settle. How she was both hungry and had no appetite at the same time. It was familiar. It was a distant memory, but still. It was exactly how it felt all those years ago when Brandon Ryan had gone to school the day after their date, when she hadn't let him stick his hands down her pants the way it was rumored he'd done with all the other girls, and told everyone that not only had Natalie let him, but she'd also had sex with him. More than once.

By the time she'd walked to her locker that morning, everyone knew the story. The lie. But no one cared that it wasn't true. Not even her friends. In fact, it was Natalie's *best friend* who was the first one to say it. *Natalie Collins is a slut. A whore. She'll spread her legs for everyone.*

The fact that she hadn't done anything didn't matter. Not to anyone but her, and Natalie swore that she wouldn't open her legs for anyone. Until it mattered. Until *he* mattered.

And she had.

Or so she'd thought.

"Natalie?"

Jason's voice broke through her thoughts. She lifted her head.

"You were off an hour ago. You going home?"

Home? There was really no other place to go, not that she wanted to tell Jason that. But if she went home, she'd be alone with her thoughts and so far they hadn't gotten her anywhere. She'd contemplated calling Sarah, but the doctor's office she worked at didn't close for another hour or so, and she didn't want to bother her at work.

"Yes," she said after a moment. "I probably am."

Jason gave her a strange look, as if he were about to ask more about it, but then his smile was back. "I also wanted to let you know that the first class went well this afternoon."

Class?

Oh. It was Tuesday. Of course. After her humiliating morning at Aiden's house, Natalie had spent most of Sunday burying her head in her pillow and feeling sorry for herself, but she managed to pull it out long enough to text Jason and ask him to take over the first wilderness first-aid class that she'd committed to teaching to Aiden's Outdoor Ed class later that week.

She'd totally forgotten.

Natalie managed to put what she hoped was a genuine smile on her face. "I hope it went well," she said. "And I really do appreciate you taking it over for me. You're probably better suited to it anyway." For so many reasons. The least of which was the fact that Jason grew up in the mountains and had far superior experience than Natalie when it came to the subject. She really had no business teaching the class to a group of high school kids.

"I appreciate your vote of confidence." He smiled. "And I was wondering if you wanted to grab a drink and maybe I could recap where I left off. So, you know, you'll know where things are at for class on Thursday."

"Wait. What?"

Jason ducked his head down and shrugged a little. "Sorry if I'm being a bit presumptuous, but I guess I just assumed since you wanted me to take today's class and...well... I know you were sort of dating Aiden, but if you're not now, then maybe—"

"No." She interrupted him with a wave of a hand. It was true she definitely didn't want to talk about those particular details with Jason, but there were more pressing matters. "Thursday? What do you mean? I thought you were taking the class."

He pressed his lips together and shook his head in a quick apology. "Sorry. I have to take my mother into the city Thursday for an appointment and the other classes don't line up either. I was scheduled before—"

"So you can't teach the class?"

He shook his head again. "No. I didn't realize you wanted me to take it completely."

But if Jason couldn't do it, and the chief wanted to make it a *club*, she'd have to do it. And then she'd have to see Aiden... and in a *high school*, of all places. She groaned, and only belatedly realized she'd done it out loud.

"I am sorry, Nat." He waited a beat. "How about that beer?"

Natalie hadn't shown up to teach the class.

It had been three days since their disastrous *morning after*. Three days that he'd stewed and played the events over and over in his head.

Was there something he could have done differently?

Absolutely.

There was *so* much he could have done differently. Like, everything.

He was still upset. But damn, he missed Natalie. A lot.

More than once, Aiden had picked up his phone to text her or call her, just so he could hear her voice and they could figure everything out and hopefully…*what?*

Move on? Get past it? Pretend it didn't happen?

She'd lied to him.

Maybe not overtly, but withholding the truth like that was almost the same. Especially the truth that she'd withheld.

A virgin?

Hell. That wasn't fair to keep that from him. And why would she? If they were getting as close as he thought they were…why wouldn't she trust him with that information?

Every time he thought about that night and how he'd…a growl of frustration rose inside him. He'd been so rough with her. He'd let his need and desire for her overshadow everything and if he'd known that…*shit.*

The fact that Aiden hadn't told her about Brenna…well, that was different. *Wasn't it?*

It was a part of his life he was trying to put behind him. It didn't have anything to do with who he was now.

Maybe Natalie felt the same?

He couldn't think clearly.

With classes over for the day, Aiden packed up his things, leaving the stack of unmarked papers on his desk. They could wait. He was in no state for marking. He needed some fresh air. No. He needed a drink. Hell, he needed both, because every time he thought about that night with Natalie, he was conflicted. Without a doubt, it had been the most connected he'd ever felt with a woman. *Ever.* It was no contest. And the sex…damn. Out of this world. And that was the problem. How could he be both angry at himself and full of shame for the way he'd taken her and at the same time feel that it had been absolutely perfect and the hottest sex he'd ever had?

He needed out of his head.

Aiden drove the short distance to his house, but instead of going inside, he left his car parked out front and walked toward Main Street. It was a warm spring day. The snow was melting and almost gone in places that the afternoon sun hit. He unzipped his jacket and let the air hit his face as he took deep breaths. By the time he got to Main Street, he felt better. Not that it was much of an improvement.

"Hey…Aiden, right?"

"Nick." Aiden automatically smiled at the man he'd almost ran into on the sidewalk. He'd been so lost in his own thoughts he hadn't even seen him pushing the stroller. "Sorry, man. I almost crashed right into you."

"All good." Nick laughed. "I've been there myself."

"Been where?"

"So twisted up about a girl that you can't think straight."
What?

Aiden was about to protest when Nick added, "Of course, the *girl* who had me twisted up is a chubby-cheeked little angel with the sweetest smile." He bent down and tickled the little girl who giggled the sweetest sound and kicked her feet. It was so cute that Aiden couldn't help but smile.

"Wow."

"Right?" Nick said. "I have never met another female who has the power to make me smile the way she does. Magical, right?"

Aiden had met one other woman who could put a smile on

his face just as easily. Maybe even more so. But she also apparently had the power to take it away just as quickly. His smile twisted into a frown he felt deep in his gut.

"Hey," Nick said. "Sorry, man. I didn't mean to—"

"Is this some sort of *new in town* meet-up?" Jeremy Davis, his hands full of boxes from Sweetie Pies, joined them on the sidewalk.

"If it were…"

Jeremy laughed. "I know, I know—then I'm out. But I could bribe you with a cinnamon bun."

"Any honey buns?" Aiden was a sucker for those buns, even if they did make him think of Natalie. But everything made him think of her, so what did it matter?

"Sorry, just cinnamon today."

Aiden shook his head. "I'm out."

Jeremy looked to Nick, who shook his head firmly. "Not today. I gotta keep my sexy dad bod if I have any hope of ever dating again."

Something flickered on Jeremy's face, but his friendly grin didn't falter. "And are you thinking of dating again?" Aiden didn't miss the edge to his words. "With everything you have going on with Amelia and getting settled in a new town and all?"

"I think I can manage it all." Nick's smile was friendly. If he noticed a change in Jeremy, he wasn't showing it. "In fact, I'm considering new investments I can get involved with. Maybe a business." His eyes moved down the street to the Knot, which was still Aiden's destination.

A cold beer was sounding more and more like a plan.

"You're going to buy the Knot? A bar?" Jeremy's mouth fell open. "Is that really the best—"

Nick laughed. "No. I'm not going to buy a bar. That's crazy. But I was thinking a cold beer on the patio might be a nice treat this afternoon." He looked at the men. "Anyone interested?"

"It's like you read my mind."

But Jeremy shook his head. "Another time. I need to get these back to the station."

He moved to leave but before he got too far, Nick asked another question. "How's your sister? Is she...I mean..."

Jeremy froze and turned around slowly. This time there was no mistaking the caution in the fire chief's eyes. "She's as good as can be expected," he said. "It's going to take time for her to be one hundred percent, you know?"

Nick nodded while Aiden looked between the two of them. He'd heard rumors of Charlotte, Jeremy's sister, fleeing a controlling relationship out East before coming back home to Glacier Falls, but he didn't know much more than that.

"Of course," Nick said. "I get it. Tell her I said hi, okay?"

Jeremy swallowed hard, but nodded. "Have a good day, guys."

Aiden doubted very much that he could, but he returned the sentiment before walking the short distance toward the Knot with Nick. But when they got to the pub, Aiden froze. His eyes went directly to the sunny patio, where a few patrons had already claimed tables. Among them was Natalie.

A million feelings, none of which Aiden wanted to deal with in public in front of everyone, flooded his senses. Instinctively, he took a step backward.

"You know what?" He shook his head and backed away. "I don't think a beer is a good idea."

Confusion lined Nick's face as he examined Aiden. But when his gaze followed to where Aiden's eyes were locked, on Natalie, who'd also seen him and was staring back with a matching look on her face, his expression morphed into one of understanding. "I see."

"You don't."

"I do."

Aiden turned to him, only reluctantly taking his eyes off Natalie, who was watching him. He'd seen hurt in her eyes, too. And the way that simple look sent sensations through his body threatened to overwhelm him. If he didn't get control, Aiden was afraid he might do something he'd regret. Or maybe he should just let those feelings take over and see what happened. Anything was better than this hell he was currently in.

"You have no idea—"

"Look, man. We just met, so I'm not going to pretend to know you or what's going on here. But I'm not stupid and I'm definitely not blind, and neither is anyone else here. It's a small town and I may still be new, but I know enough to know that in Glacier Falls, your business is *everyone's* business. That woman in there." He gestured with his shoulder. "Is feeling whatever it is you're feeling. I'm not going to ask what happened. It's none of my business. And I'm not going to pretend that I know what it's like to be in love like that, because I don't. But I've seen it happen more than once, and I've also seen perfectly intelligent men and women almost throw it all away because they can't get over some stupid bullshit thing. Story as old as time." He crossed his arms and raised his eyebrows to make his point.

It was made.

Sure, Nick had oversimplified it, and he didn't know a thing about Aiden or his past with women who lied to him and used him, and how he felt about complete honesty in a relationship and moreover…how *he'd* screwed up, too. Still…he had a point.

Aiden took a breath and turned to look once again at Natalie. She was gorgeous. The way the sun hit her face lit her up. But it also clearly showed him her eyes. The hurt and hope reflected there hit him in the gut and made him almost physically ill.

He loved her.

It hit him like a physical blow. *He loved her.* And that's why it hurt so damn much. He hadn't felt this way about anyone before. Not even Brenna when he married her.

And that's what stopped him.

He'd loved before. Not nearly as hard as he was loving now, and that had ended badly. *So* badly. He'd only just barely recovered. And what he felt for Natalie was *so* much stronger. But Natalie had lied, too. She'd kept things from him...but so had he...*why*? They'd both screwed up. So why did he react the way he had? Why had he flown off the handle like that? He was better than that. They could have talked it through, and started fresh, with everything out in the open, but he'd been so quick to shut down.

Why?

He knew the answer.

Defense.

Just like in hockey when he was a kid. The best defense was a strong offense.

He'd seen a crack that meant he could be hurt, so he'd attacked.

He was an idiot.

A full-scale, giant idiot of the worst kind.

He needed to talk to her. He needed to make it all better. This was too much. This distance. Even after only three days, it was too much.

Somewhere beside him, Aiden registered that Nick was there. He was saying something about relationships and his friend Damon and...Aiden tuned him out. Focused only on Natalie.

He was about to go to her, to repair the crack in their new relationship before it could split wide open, when he saw *him*. Another man, who looked vaguely familiar to Aiden. He stepped out onto the patio, carrying two beers. He set one in front of Natalie before taking a seat next to her. She turned and smiled at the other man. She *smiled*. Jealousy and hurt and confusion and so much more tumbled through him until Aiden couldn't see straight. It had only been three days and she'd already moved on?

And after what they'd shared…

It was too much. He stepped backward, needing distance.

"Aiden? Are you—"

"I have to go." He shook his head and moved to leave. "I can't be here."

Aiden didn't wait for Nick's response before he tore his gaze away from Natalie's, shoved his hands in his pockets, and walked away. It was the only thing he could do.

Chapter Sixteen

AIDEN.

The moment she saw him, everything else faded away. It was as if she'd been waiting three whole days to lay eyes on him again. Like a fix her body and soul needed. And now...

He was walking away.

No.

"Natalie?"

Vaguely, she registered Jason's voice. She forced herself to look away from Aiden's retreating form and back to her friend.

"Are you okay?" Jason watched her with a look that, at first glance, she was sure was concern. But then he pressed his lips together and shook his head. "He doesn't deserve you."

"What?" She shook her head, confused by the change in him. "What do you mean?"

"That guy." He shrugged dismissively. "If he can't see what an amazing woman you are, he doesn't deserve you."

Natalie looked back to where Aiden had been standing. Nick Newton and his baby were now also headed in the same direction Aiden had gone. She turned back to Jason, who was sipping his beer with a satisfied smirk on his face.

Jason had no idea what had happened between them. How she'd lied. How she'd discovered *his* lie. The way they'd spoken to each other. The hurt. The...passion. There was that, too. She couldn't allow herself to forget that either. The way he'd made her feel and the connection they had. It was there. It was real. And it was special. She knew that in her heart. "What do you mean?" she asked. "You don't know what happened."

Her friend and co-worker's face softened, the self-satisfied edge gone. "No," he said much more kindly. "I don't. And you're right, I shouldn't jump to conclusions. But..." Jason sighed and scrubbed a hand over his face. "I might as well just say it."

"Say what?"

"It can't be a secret that I have kind of a *thing* for you, right?"

Natalie remembered the conversation that Jeremy had with her not long ago. *He has a crush on you.* But it *had* come as a surprise to her, because she was so oblivious to these things. Still, she nodded.

"Well, I'll be honest," Jason continued. "I thought I still had a chance, but when I saw you two together at Jeremy's party, I realized..." He shook his head and let out a low whistle.

Natalie tipped her head, confused but needing to hear more.

"No one stood a chance," he finished. "No one besides him. The two of you together...well, you don't see that every day."

"You don't?" Natalie was acutely aware that she was probably sounding oddly every bit the inexperienced woman she was, but she no longer cared. There was only one thing she cared about, and he was walking away.

"No, Nat." Jason's voice was kind. "I'm no love guru, but I do know enough to know that you don't see that kind of connection every day. And if *I* noticed it, then I can't even imagine what the two of...but, I guess it doesn't matter, because my point is that any guy who would walk away from a connection like that...especially one with *you*..." He shook his head. "He doesn't deserve you."

She let his words circle around and around in her head. Finally she said, "But what if I did the same thing?"

"You walked away?"

She remembered back to Sunday morning, when she'd been the one to run out of his house, wearing nothing more than her coat over his shirt and bare legs. What if she'd stayed? Would they have talked? Would they have been able to get past...*dammit.*

She would never know because she hadn't stayed.

"I did." Natalie shook her head, but jumped up from the table. "But I won't do it again." She grabbed her purse and her sweater. At the last minute, she turned to Jason. "I'm sorry. And thank you. I..."

"Go." His smile was sad, but resigned.

There was nothing else she could say. She nodded and ran down the patio steps until she was on the sidewalk.

She couldn't see him. He'd gone east. Away from the direction of his house, but...Natalie scanned the street and finally guessed. She hoped like hell her guess was right as she started jogging.

She'd been stupid and yes, she could blame her inexperience and her past. But she'd been doing that for too long, and she didn't want to live in the past anymore. She didn't want everything that had happened when she was in high school to dictate how she was living now.

And she sure as hell didn't want to lose what could very well be the best thing that had ever walked into her life because of it.

No.

She pushed herself harder. She couldn't lose him.

And then...*Aiden*.

"Aiden!" she yelled through her breathlessness. Natalie stopped running and dropped her hands to her knees, pulling in air and trying to catch her breath before looking up and calling out again, "Aiden!"

When she yelled the second time, he heard her and turned.

"Aiden, I..." She could hardly get the words out as she gasped for breath. Clearly she needed to work on her cardio if she planned to chase men down the street.

But not *men*. Just one. And she'd chase him as long as it took. She knew that now with a clarity that would have scared her if it wasn't so damn exciting.

He walked toward her.

"Nat? What are...are you..."

She nodded as her breathing finally started to return to normal, although she was certain she'd feel the burn in her lungs for a while yet. "Aiden. I need to...why did you walk away?"

Natalie certainly hadn't planned to ask him that. But to be fair, she hadn't planned anything at all, and suddenly it became important to know. If what Jason had said was true, or even if there were a thread of truth to it, then why had he walked away from her?

"Truth?"

She nodded. "Always."

The urge to reach out to him, to touch him was a physical pull that caused an aching in her entire body.

"When I saw you sitting there, I was..." He looked down for a moment. "I wanted more than anything to talk to you, to...but then..." He shook his head. "I want you to be happy, Natalie. More than anything else, I want you to be happy, and when I saw that you were with..." He sucked in a breath and shook his head again. "I can't stand in the way of your happiness. You deserve to have a relationship that's open and free and honest. And so do I. And if we can't do that…if that can't be with me, then—"

"It *can* be with you." She almost yelled the words. Panic filled her. He wasn't saying what he was saying. He couldn't be, because he was wrong. "Aiden." Natalie tried desperately to control the panic building inside. "I can be happy and open and honest and all those things with you." Tears filled her eyes and spilled unchecked down her cheeks as she shook her head. "And maybe I didn't tell you one thing, but that didn't mean I wasn't happy. No. That's wrong." She swallowed hard. "Aiden, I *am* happy with you. Happier than I've ever been in my whole life."

The irony of what she was saying while simultaneously falling completely apart struck her as funny and she laughed a little as a sob escaped her. The resulting choking sound filled the space between them. She wiped her face and tried again. "Maybe I should say that I *was* happy with you." She tried to smile but he was watching her with an expression she couldn't read; it was starting to crack her heart wide open. "Aiden, I don't know what happened with us or how it went so wrong so quickly. Maybe I should have told you I was a virgin. Honestly, I didn't think it would matter and that it was my own personal thing to know, but—"

Aiden's brain was very quickly catching up to what was happening. But not quick enough, because he was still having a whole hell of a lot of trouble processing that Natalie was standing in front of him. She was out of breath. She'd run.

To him.

Dammit. He should have been the one doing the running

to her. He was an idiot. But he'd meant what he'd said. More than anything, he wanted her to be happy.

She was talking. "Aiden, I *am* happy with you. Happier than I've ever been in my whole life."

But how? With everything that had happened after the best night of his life, how could that have made her happy? She deserved so much better.

"Maybe I should say that I *was* happy with you."

Those words killed him. If he could rewind the last few days and start it over, he would literally give *everything*.

"Aiden, I don't know what happened with us or how it went so wrong so quickly. Maybe I should have told you I was a virgin. Honestly, I didn't think it would matter and that it was my own personal thing to know, but—"

"No. You didn't owe that to me. I had no right to get upset with you. I just…"

He couldn't stand it one more second. She'd probably push him away or slap him, but he didn't care. He'd take whatever she could dish out. Aiden reached out and pulled her tight to him before crushing her lips with his.

He needed to taste her. He needed to feel her. He needed to know whether he could be the one to make her happy.

Startled, she didn't immediately melt into his embrace. But then, a small moan and he felt the moment she let go.

He twined her hair through his hands, and as if his entire future depended on it—which maybe it did—he tried to convey every little bit of what he was feeling into that one moment.

When finally he pulled away, she looked up at him. Her lips parted, her breath coming in pants, no longer from the running, and her eyes held a question.

"Natalie." Her name came out rough, almost choked. "I… everything that I said…that I did…" He couldn't even stand it.

He'd been terrible. He'd been mad at *her*. For what? For his own insecurities.

He probably should have given her space, but he couldn't bear to not touch her. He kept one hand on her back, holding her close to him, and his other hand traced down her cheek. "*I* want to be the one to make you happy." He'd never meant anything more. "And I think I can."

She nodded slowly. "I *know* you can." Her head dipped. "I'm so sorry, Aiden. I should have—"

He held a finger to her mouth. "No. Never apologize. You didn't need to tell me. You didn't owe me that. I'm the one who should be apologizing. I never should have gotten upset with you. I panicked."

A tear slipped down her cheek, but he wiped it away and made a silent vow never to be the cause of her tears again. Ever.

"You panicked?"

"Yes," he said slowly. "It wasn't fair of me not to tell you about Brenna and..." He swallowed hard. Even though he'd finally come to the realization, it was still hard for him to say. "I meant to and then....it doesn't matter. I should have. And then, that morning, it was all too much to know that I'd kept something from you, and you'd kept something from me. And what I really want is a relationship with you that's completely honest. No secrets. And I was afraid that if we started out this way that—"

"You want a relationship?"

He nodded and slid his hands down her sides until he was holding her forearms.

He was vaguely aware that they stood in the middle of the sidewalk where everyone in town could see them, but he didn't care. He had a few things he needed to say to Natalie, and he had no plans to move until he'd said them.

"I do. Very much. I want a relationship built on honesty

and trust. I've been hurt in the past, Nat, and I thought that this could be different. And then that morning…" He shook his head and dropped his chin to his chest. "I was wrong."

Confusion lined her face, and immediately he regretted his choice of words. "No. I don't mean it like that. I don't mean that I was wrong about having that kind of relationship or having it with you." He shook his head. "Never. Not even for a second."

Natalie tilted her head and eyed him. "Then what?"

"I was wrong that one misunderstanding could or should destroy what could be a very amazing thing between us. I was wrong to think that ignoring it and pushing you away was the right thing. And I'm so sorry I didn't tell you about Brenna long before then."

Something flickered in her eyes and she took a deep breath. "Just the way I should have told you my secret."

It still pained Aiden to think about the way he'd treated her first time. He would never forgive himself for that. He should have done it differently. He should have made it…but… "No." He shook his head softly. "That's different. You didn't have to tell me that. It's…but can I ask why you didn't tell me?" There was something she'd said at the time. A flicker of a memory. A reason.

Her lips twitched up into a tiny smile before it vanished again. "I didn't want you to treat me any differently," she said. "I didn't want it to be a *thing* between us. I just know I wanted you, and I wanted it to be *real* and in the moment."

It definitely was that.

"It wasn't about keeping secrets," she said. "Not really. I just…"

He touched his finger to her lips. "No more secrets, okay?"

"No more secrets." She smiled and then dropped her chin quickly before looking away.

"Tell me what you're thinking." Aiden lifted her chin with his finger so they could look each other in the eyes. "Please."

Natalie swallowed hard. "I'm thinking that I've never felt the way I've felt when I'm with you and...I'm afraid I might be in love with you."

Her words tore through him, leaving him in tatters. But also, they gave him strength. "You're afraid?"

She nodded.

"Don't be afraid."

Natalie laughed a little. "How could I not be? I've never felt this way before and we've managed to—"

He cut her off with another kiss, because there was no way Aiden was going to let her finish that sentence. They had *not* screwed anything up. They were humans. Imperfect humans who made mistakes and then fixed them. And they'd do it together as long as she'd let him. Because as long as they did it together, they'd be okay. Better than okay.

They'd be together. That's all he needed. And everything he wanted.

Chapter Seventeen

NATALIE COULDN'T CONVINCE herself to open her eyes. The last time she'd woken up in Aiden's bed, she'd been filled with a joy like she'd never felt before. But only for a moment before it was ripped away.

Of course, they'd not actually fallen asleep this time. As far as she knew, it was probably around eight or nine at night.

Still.

She'd already laid there with her eyes squeezed shut, trying her best not to be superstitious for far too long.

Reasonably, she knew there was nothing to be afraid of: before they'd finally tumbled into Aiden's bed, no longer able to keep their hands and mouths off each other, they'd talked about *everything*. They'd both apologized so many times for overreacting, Natalie was sure they'd worn out the words. But the more they talked, the more she understood his reaction the other morning when she freaked out about Brenna.

And he understood her reaction.

And most importantly, they both understood that they'd both acted like idiots. Idiots who were obviously so terrified and overwhelmed by the feelings stirred up in their souls that they'd overreacted. Terribly overreacted.

Thankfully, they'd been able to move past it and into the making up part of the evening. Natalie's body still vibrated from all of the *making up* they'd done. Still, she wouldn't open her eyes.

"Nat?"

"No." She shook her head against the pillow as Aiden slid his hand over her bare midsection and slowly started drawing circles on her belly.

He laughed. "What are you saying no to?"

"No to waking up."

"You weren't sleeping."

"Doesn't matter."

"Umm…it kind of does."

She heard the humor in his voice, but still, she squeezed her eyes shut. She loved where they were now. The way things were. *She didn't think she'd be able to survive if—* Her thoughts dissolved as Natalie felt the bed shift as Aiden joined her. Still, she kept her eyes shut tight.

"You're just being silly, now."

"Am I?"

"You are." He kissed each of her closed eyelids. "You must be starving. As much as I like you here, exactly as you are in this moment, I should feed you."

Her stomach rumbled. The idea of food did sound good.

"But if I open my eyes, what if…" She swallowed back her own foolishness. "What if it goes away again?"

Aiden groaned in understanding. "Like last time."

It wasn't a question, but Natalie nodded.

She knew she was being foolish and so very childish. Even so, Aiden didn't try to make her feel that way.

Instead, with a tender, yet commanding voice, he said,

"Open your eyes, Natalie. Look at me." When she didn't immediately open them, he added, "Please."

She couldn't resist him. Finally, she fluttered her eyes open and they locked immediately on his deep-brown eyes, that looked almost black the way they bored into her with so much intensity it made her entire body shiver.

"See?" His voice was a whisper. "It's still okay. *We're* still okay."

She nodded. "We are."

"We are."

He was pressed up against her, so there was no way she could miss the way he twitched against her, once more stirring to life with desire.

"We are," she said again and wiggled her hips a little.

Aiden groaned. "And you know exactly what you do to me."

She bit her bottom lip. It was still very new to her, this feeling, and knowing she could elicit the same in him was a heady feeling.

"And not only are we okay," he said with a kiss. "We're going to be more than okay." He kissed her again, longer this time. "Much more than okay."

Natalie took a deep breath, filling her lungs.

"Do you believe me?"

She nodded. "One hundred percent."

Aiden shifted over her, moving his body so that his once again hard length was pressed against the cleft between her legs. They'd only just finished making love, but it didn't matter. Natalie didn't think she would ever get tired of it and the need he'd woken in her. He looked in her eyes, and she nodded slightly before lifting her hips in welcome.

When he pressed into her, it took Natalie's breath away, the way it always did. He kissed her as he moved slowly over her.

Slower than he ever had before. A tear slipped down her cheek and when Aiden noticed it, he froze.

"Nat, I—"

She smiled and laughed. "It's good. I'm good. I promise. I'm just so…"

He waited.

"I'm happy." The words came out in a rush of tears, which made her feel ridiculous, but she couldn't have stopped them if she tried. When concerned, Aiden tried to shift off her, but Natalie gripped his buttocks. "No."

Somehow she managed to wrap a leg around him and in a quick movement, she used it for leverage to flip him so he was on his back and she was now in control. His wide eyes registered as much surprise as she felt at what had just happened.

"I never…wow."

Natalie bent down to kiss him hard. "I told you," she said between kisses. "I'm happy." And then, taking control of that happiness, she showed him exactly how happy they both could be.

Somehow Aiden had managed to pull himself away from Natalie and his bed, and move into the kitchen. They were both starving and exhausted. It had been an intense afternoon, full of *all* the feelings. More than he even knew he was capable of. But as with a lot of things with Natalie, she somehow taught him things that he never knew about himself. Like, most importantly, his huge capacity to love someone as much as he loved her.

And it was only the beginning.

Their love was only going to grow, of that he was sure.

Aiden glanced to where Natalie sat at the table, devouring

the plate of toast and scrambled eggs he'd made for her. "Are you sure you're ready?"

She looked up, her fork halfway to her mouth. Her smile lit up her face and she nodded eagerly. "So ready."

Aiden laughed as he took the cup out of the espresso machine and carried it to the table.

"Finally," she said with an exaggerated wave of her arms. "I feel like I've been waiting my whole life for this life-changing coffee."

He'd promised her, when they'd finished making love—again—that he wouldn't let her leave without actually making her a cup of the coffee. Not that he wanted her to leave at all. In fact, if Aiden had his way, neither of them would leave his house until they ran out of food and needed to go for supplies. But as amazing as it sounded in theory, he knew it wouldn't happen. At least not this week.

He set the coffee in front of her. "I'm glad you're ready," he said dramatically. "Because this coffee will change your life."

She picked up the cup, but paused when it was almost to her lips. "You know, this could change *everything*."

He nodded seriously.

She winked and took a small sip of the steaming drink. Aiden watched as she closed her eyes and made a soft moaning noise that, so far, she'd reserved for their time in bed together. Irrationally, he felt a spark of jealousy. She lifted her shoulders in exaggerated delight and when she finally opened her eyes again, there was a twinkle in them. "You were right. My life is completely changed." She set the cup down and shrugged. "Everything looks different." She stood and moved to the middle of the room, where she spun around with her arms outstretched, like a little girl. "It's like I can see for the first time."

"Okay, okay." He joined her in the middle of the room and

wrapped his arms around her. "It's not *that* kind of life changing."

"Maybe not," she said with a giggle as he held her tight. "But you are."

It was such an unexpected thing for her to say. He was at a loss for words.

"Not like anything or anyone I've had before," Natalie said softly. "You've completely changed my life."

A flood of warmth and love flowed through him. He nodded slowly. "The same way you've changed mine."

They kissed in the middle of the kitchen floor before Aiden led Nat back to the kitchen table so they could finish their meals. The sooner they finished, the sooner he could take her back to bed. But there was one more thing he needed to know.

When they were almost done eating, Aiden finally asked the question he'd been wanting the answer for. "Will you tell me why you waited?"

She didn't seem surprised at all by the question. Natalie nodded, put down her fork, and took her time answering.

Aiden knew there was more to it than simply waiting for the *right one*, and he wasn't surprised when she told him about the bullying in high school or the rumors. Reflexively, his fists clenched under the table at the mention of the boy who'd hurt her. A selfish, immature boy who hadn't gotten what he wanted from her and so had set out to ruin her. She spoke without emotion, as if it were a fact she'd accepted long ago. Which it obviously was. But Aiden's heart ached for the girl who'd been hurt so badly and had missed so much.

But the ache melted when he saw the way Natalie responded to the story. "It wasn't so much that I was going to wait until marriage," she used air quotes, "or anything," Natalie continued. "I just wanted to wait until I met someone who was...well, who was *worth* it."

Aiden couldn't help but be honored by her choice of words.

"And then I guess I got kind of busy going to school and working, and I was focused on my career and...well, it's hard to find someone worthy when you're not looking."

"You weren't looking when you met me." He grinned and winked, and she laughed.

"No." She shook her head. "I was not looking for you. But I sure am glad I found you." She left her seat and walked around the table to him, where Aiden pulled her onto his lap to kiss her again.

Their lips would be swollen and bruised in the morning, but he didn't care because he would happily spend the rest of his life proving to Natalie that he was worthy of her, and he planned to keep it that way.

Chapter Eighteen

"WHAT'S THE INJURY?" Natalie knelt in the now mostly green grass in the school field, next to the student who held another student's bandaged and splinted arm.

"The wrist appears to be broken," the student said seriously. "Or seriously sprained."

Natalie nodded and waited.

"The injury has been splinted with some firm sticks and a length of cloth from a shirt." Natalie narrowed her eyes in question, and the student quickly added, "From an undershirt. I tried to make sure it was as clean as possible as there was also a cut on the arm and I want to avoid infection."

Nat smiled and pushed up from the grass, the knees of her pants soaked through. "Good work, Ben. I think you got it."

Ben smiled and did a fist pump before high-fiving the student he'd just finished *treating* for his *injured* hand.

Natalie laughed and shook her head. The wilderness first-aid club had been a hit with the students, who'd all signed up on their own, and with Natalie. She'd really enjoyed teaching, especially when they were able to get out of the classroom and outside.

Her hatred for high schools had diminished somewhat in the last few weeks. Dating a sexy school teacher had a lot to do with it, but some of the old feelings still lingered.

But those were about the only old feelings that lingered these days, because everything was feeling brand-new.

"Great work today, everyone."

Natalie turned to Aiden, who was the number-one reason that everything felt so new *and* so damn good. And just like every time she looked at him, she smiled.

In fact, Natalie couldn't seem to stop smiling these days, and it wasn't a problem she cared to *fix*.

She moved through the kids who were still all sitting on the grass in their pairs with their various fake injuries that Natalie had assigned. It *had* been a great class. The students had jumped at the opportunity to practice everything they'd learned over the last few weeks; when Nat came up with the idea to give them situations to act out, they'd loved it.

And they'd all done really well.

As Nat joined Aiden, where he stood off to the side of the field, she felt that swell of pride in the students that he'd once described was the best part of his job. Naturally, she grabbed his hand to squeeze it before remembering they were in front of a group of teenagers and she pulled away quickly.

"It's okay," one of the girls, Simone, the girl who on the very first day of class recognized Natalie, said as she returned the supplies to the bin in front of them. "We all know you two are dating." Simone winked. "Thank you, Natalie. This was a really great class."

"Hey." Aiden pretended to be offended. "I was your teacher."

Simone shrugged with typical teenage disinterest. "Whatever."

When she walked away, Aiden reached for her hand and squeezed quickly before returning his attention to the rest of the kids who were all returning their supplies as well. When the last bandage was back in the box, he glanced at his watch. "We should get going, Nat. We're going to be late, and you still need to change."

They knew they were pushing it to hold the *field dressing* session of the club on the Saturday before Hope and Levi's baby celebration party. But the students had been eager, and Aiden hadn't wanted to stifle any of that excitement because, as he said, "It's hard to get them excited about much that isn't on their phones these days." So they'd made it happen.

But Aiden was right; Natalie still had to change out of her jeans and maybe do something with her hair before they got to the party at Ever After Ranch. She'd been beyond honored to even be invited to baby Cole's naming ceremony. They weren't calling it a baptism or christening, as Hope and Levi had decided to raise their baby with spiritualness and an under-standing of all religions, but they did feel it was important to have a proper welcoming of their son to the world.

Natalie thought it all sounded beautiful. And from the moment she got the invitation as a person of honor, she'd been looking forward to the day.

"It'll only take me a minute," she told Aiden as they got in his car and drove the short distance to his place. The night before, she'd taken her change of clothes to his house because, well...she'd largely been spending most of her time there anyway. His rental was starting to feel more and more like home, even in the few short weeks since they'd been officially dating. Although she still hadn't figured out how to work the coffee machine.

While Natalie was in the bathroom trying to wrangle her hair into some type of suitable style, Aiden had changed into a fresh pair of black dress pants and a bright-green shirt that he'd left unbuttoned at the collar instead of a tie. After all, it was meant to be a casual affair.

She paused in the door when she realized he was on a phone call. His back was turned to her, so he didn't see her standing there, nor did he see the way her knees buckled a little, or the way her hand reached out to brace herself from the hurt, when he said, "No, Brenna. She doesn't know yet."

Aiden had been naive when he thought he was done with his ex-wife. He'd sent in his last payment. He'd even sent it early. After everything that had gone down with Natalie, and the wake-up call he'd had about how he could very well have lost the best thing that had ever happened to him, he'd sat her down and told her all about his first marriage.

He'd told Nat everything. Not leaving out any detail. He needed her to know and to understand how much he'd changed, and how he wasn't the same man who had married Brenna and let himself be used the way he was. More than that, though, he wanted Natalie to understand that there was nothing he would keep from her. Not again.

He'd sent Brenna one last message, letting her know that they were done. He wouldn't be answering her calls anymore and she needed to move on the same way he had.

When Aiden hadn't heard back from her, he'd assumed it was over. Finally.

And then the phone rang.

His heart had sunk when he saw Brenna's name on the screen. He muttered a curse under his breath and almost didn't answer at all. But he knew if he didn't, she'd just keep trying. There was one thing that would end it all for good.

He answered the call. "Brenna."

"Lover." Her voice dripped with insincerity. "I'm glad I caught you. I need you to deposit—"

"No." He wanted to keep it simple. "We're done, Brenna. I

sent your last payment last week. Remember? I sent you an email letting you know that the payment was early and we were done."

"But I didn't get—"

"You did." He forced himself to keep his voice calm and even. "I have the confirmation from the bank that you accepted it."

"But Aiden, I—"

"No." He cut her off. "We're done, Brenna. It's over. Like I said in my last message to you, please don't contact me anymore. As far as I'm concerned, we're done here. I'm seeing someone new now and I've moved on with my life."

"You're what? That woman who answered the phone? You're not serious?"

"I am. Very serious."

Aiden knew that would be the final straw for her. Breanna had always harbored some sort of misguided delusion that the reason Aiden wasn't dating anyone was because he secretly still loved and wanted her. It couldn't have been further from the truth, and now she'd finally understand that. Some exes would have turned that into a challenge, but Aiden knew Brenna wouldn't. She was a lot of things, but she wouldn't subject herself to being rejected because there was someone new in his life. He knew that with certainty.

"More importantly, we're both very serious," he added. It wasn't a lie. He was *very* serious about Natalie. And he hoped like hell she was, too. "I'm going to ask her to marry me." He said it aloud before he even realized what he was doing. But the moment it came out of his mouth, he knew it was true. He *was* going to ask. It didn't matter that they'd only been together a few weeks. When you knew, you knew.

And he *knew*.

On the other end of the line, he heard Brenna exhale slowly and he knew she understood. "Does she know?"

Aiden turned and looked out the window at the mountains he'd come to love as his new home. "No, Brenna." He shook his head. "She doesn't know yet."

He turned, and the smile on his face dissolved at the sight of the woman he loved. She looked gorgeous in her white dress, covered in bright, spring-like flowers. Her blonde hair tumbled over her shoulder, but his eyes went straight to her face—and the fear and sadness and hurt he saw there.

Shit.

She'd heard him.

But how much had she heard?

He shook his head and looked straight in Natalie's eyes. He needed her to understand that it wasn't what she thought it was. Because he was pretty sure she thought it was bad. And it wasn't. It really wasn't.

"It's all done now, Brenna," he said into the phone, while holding Natalie's stare. "Don't contact me again."

He didn't wait to hear her response before hanging up. He dropped the phone to the coffee table and walked straight over to the love of his life. Aiden put his hands on her hips and held her firm. "Do you want to know what you heard?"

He could see the concern and worry about what she'd heard in her eyes. Her breath came fast and he knew she had the instinct to run. But she wouldn't. Not again. They'd been through it once, and they both knew what they'd almost lost by not being able to communicate.

Never again.

"I'll tell you."

She nodded.

Aiden led her to the couch and they sat. It wasn't how he wanted to ask her. She deserved so much more than a living room proposal. But the one thing Natalie deserved more than anything else was the truth in their relationship. Always. Over everything.

"That was Brenna."

She nodded. "I got that."

"I told her about you."

Her eyes opened in surprise. "You did? Won't that make things worse? Won't she—"

"Exactly the opposite." Aiden shook his head. "She won't bother me again. She won't bother *us*." When Natalie didn't look as though she believed him, he grabbed her hand and squeezed. "She won't," he said. "She won't subject herself to that kind of rejection."

After a moment, Natalie nodded. "And what about what I don't know yet?"

He smiled, despite the suspicious way she was looking at him. "Do you trust me?"

She didn't hesitate. "You know I do."

He could have left it there, but again, Aiden knew it wasn't worth it to have any questions between them. Everything needed to be out in the open. "I told her that I was going to ask you to marry me." He watched her closely while he said the words, so he didn't miss one second of the brilliant smile that lit up her face.

"You did?"

He nodded. "Of course I did."

Natalie laughed and it was such a sweet sound. Aiden needed to clear up one more thing.

"But just for the record," he said. "This isn't me asking."

Her smile dipped a little and she narrowed her eyes in question.

"Do you really think this is how I'd ask you the most important question in the world?"

There was no way. Not in a million years. Natalie deserved the best and that included a proposal worthy of how much he loved her.

"So you're not asking me…"

"Not yet." He leaned over and kissed her nose. "But I will. That's a promise."

His kiss moved lower, to her lips. He never tired of kissing her and would have happily have stayed there all day doing just that, but they had places to be.

Reluctantly, Aiden pulled back. "One more thing," he said. "I need to know you believe me about Brenna." He needed to close that chapter of his life once and for all.

Natalie nodded seriously. "I do."

He believed her. That was behind them. Now there was nothing in front of them but their future, and Aiden couldn't be more excited about what it was going to look like.

Aiden stood and offered Natalie his hand. "We should get going or we'll be late. After all, we have a baby to welcome into the world."

Chapter Nineteen

"LOOKING GOOD, guardian...or godmother...or...what do I call you?" Nick shrugged and held up his hands that were for once free of baby Amelia.

"Just call me Auntie." Steph laughed and hugged her friend. "It's good to see you."

It had only been three weeks since Steph had last been in Glacier Falls, but at times it felt as though a lifetime had passed since she'd been home. With the change of the seasons while she'd been in Los Angeles, it definitely felt like one of those times.

Spring had completely arrived in Glacier Falls. The heads of tulips and daffodils were pushing through the soil, pussy willows lined the river edge, and the green grass started to peek through. Stephanie knew enough to know that spring in the mountains could be fickle and it could still snow at any time, but it was sure hard to think of snow on such a sunny, warm day. The perfect day for baby Cole's official welcoming into the world.

Levi and Hope had decided that because neither of them had been raised with any type of formal religion but instead an overall sense of spirituality, that instead of a christening or baptism, they would hold a naming ceremony to officially welcome Cole to the world and appoint his legal guardians, as if they needed to be appointed. Faith, Logan, and Stephanie were already completely devoted to the little boy. Even from a distance, Steph tried to talk to Hope—and baby Cole—a few times a week. She hated being so far away in his early days, but she'd already vowed that his Auntie Steph would always take very good care of him.

And his mother.

Which was why she'd worked with Faith, Levi, and Logan over the last few weeks to get Hope in to see a doctor. And a good therapist. Steph hated to see her sister struggle, but with her therapist's help, as well as everyone around her who loved her, she was starting to see the light through the clouds. It didn't surprise anyone that she was struggling with post-partum depression, not really. Not with everything health-wise that she needed to deal with. It had been hard. But now she was starting to feel well enough that she was ready to have Cole's official party.

When Steph had checked in on her earlier, and Hope had given her a huge hug, the difference in her filled her heart with happiness. No doubt Hope still had a ways to go when it came to fighting those inner battles, particularly with her surgery coming up to finally help her be cancer free so she could live a long, healthy life, but Steph had no doubt she'd come through it all stronger than ever.

"I meant it," Nick said. "You look amazing. Even a few freckles peeking through." He touched Steph's nose, and she pulled away with a swat of her hand.

"You don't have to wait for spring in LA to get a little sun." She laughed. "And yes, with this red hair and fair skin, I definitely break out in freckles."

"Well, I think they're cute." Her friend grinned and turned as something—or *someone*—caught his eye.

Charlotte Davis.

"I bet that's not all you think is cute," she teased and elbowed her friend in the ribs.

"What?"

"Don't pretend you don't."

She narrowed her gaze at him, and Nick laughed. "Okay, I won't. I do think she's cute and…interesting."

"Interesting?"

He shrugged and turned back to Steph. "Every time I talk to her, I learn a little more, and I like what I'm learning. There's more to her than what's happened to her."

Steph sighed. "You know that's true of most people, right?"

Nick laughed. "Maybe so. But I'm not talking about *most people*."

"Clearly." She rolled her eyes. "So tell me something about Charlotte that you find so interesting." Steph couldn't help but egg him on a little. It wouldn't be the worst thing for him to have someone in his life.

"Did you know she's an interior designer?"

Steph shook her head; she did not know that.

"It's true. And a pretty talented one, too. Well, before she went out East anyway. But…hey! Maybe she could help you with your cabins?"

It wasn't a bad idea. Steph knew what she wanted—she just didn't know *how* to put it all together. "That could be a thing," she said. "I'll talk to her."

"Do you want to talk now? I'll go introduce you."

"Down, boy." Steph laughed again. "Besides, we've met, remember? Don't worry, I'll reach out to her and see if she has any—" Her thoughts flew from her head when her eyes landed on Travis Bishop. *What was he doing there?*

Before she could change her expression, Nick turned to see what or who she was looking at. When he turned around again, he let out a low whistle, but Steph only half noticed. She was too fixated on Travis, who looked annoyingly sexy in a clean button-down shirt, jeans that looked a little less worn-out than his usual pair, and remarkably clean, shiny black cowboy boots.

He cleaned up well.

She both hated and loved the fact that she'd even noticed.

And then he turned, his dark eyes landing on her, and a shock flew through her body.

Damn him and his effect on her.

"Maybe I'm not the only one who's found someone interesting in Glacier Falls."

Nick's teasing tone pulled Steph back into the moment. She shook her head hard and forced herself to look away from Travis. "Hardly. I've already told you, he's working on my cabins. That's it."

That wasn't it. Far from it. They'd almost—what? Kissed? *Almost.* And almost didn't count. Not that she wanted it to.

Did she?

Ugh.

Something about Travis Bishop set her on edge, and not in an entirely good way. He left her feeling unsettled and unsure. And Steph never felt that way.

She hadn't spoken to him or seen him since that day at Lynx Creek. They'd communicated by text messages and email only. The few times he had tried to call, she'd sent the call to voicemail. It was for the best. Something about his voice made her stomach flip and then she couldn't think properly and everything got all mixed up inside...

"Travis Bishop?" She tried to laugh, hoping it came off casually. "I don't think so. I mean, seriously..." Her protests didn't sound convincing even to her own ears, and judging by the look on Nick's face, he wasn't buying it either. Steph exhaled hard. "He's not even remotely my type. In fact, I don't want anything to do with Travis at all."

"Is that right?"

Her stomach flipped at the gruff voice behind her.

She turned to see Travis, looking smug and way too damn sexy in front of her. *Why did that keep happening?*

"You don't want anything to do with me?" He raised an eyebrow.

It was a challenge. What was she supposed to say?

Yes. She did want something to do with him. She wanted to kiss him. She wanted *him* to kiss her. But he hadn't. He'd more or less rejected her the last time they saw each other. She wouldn't let that happen again.

But if she said no, it would be a straight-up lie.

"I just...I was just..."

She looked to Nick for help, but he shook his head and held up his hands.

"I should go find Amelia. The women were passing her around, and she's probably getting...anyway, talk to you later." He didn't even bother finishing his excuse before running off.

Coward.

Without backup, Steph turned to Travis again and took a deep breath.

"Well?" he said. "You don't want anything to do with me?"

She exhaled slowly. "Just let it go."

He shook his head curtly. "I don't think so, because I don't think that's true at all and I'm not usually wrong about these things."

His cockiness was infuriating and incredibly sexy at the same time.

Steph took a deep breath and shook her hair back off her shoulders. "Well, you're wrong this time."

Travis took a step toward her. "So if I kissed you right now, you'd—"

"Slap you."

It was a lie. They both knew it was a lie. Still, what else could she say?

Steph hated the way her breathing was fast and hard and her palms were sweaty. Mostly, she hated that, more than anything, she wanted to pull him close and feel those lips on hers.

"Do you want to know what I think?" He didn't give her a chance to answer before he leaned in even closer. "I don't think you would."

His words were puffs of air on her lips. He was so close, she could kiss him. Would *he* kiss her?

Shit. She'd have to slap him if he did.

Steph stiffened her spine. "So test your luck then."

She didn't make the mistake of closing her eyes a second time. Instead, she stared him in the eyes until he…laughed.

He *laughed*.

Travis stepped back and put space between them.

Mercifully.

Steph gulped at the air and called on her acting training. A moment later, her face was a mask, her emotions once more under control.

"I'm glad I ran into you today."

The cockiness was gone from his voice, which shocked her more than anything else could have.

"You are?"

"Yes." His smile was slow and sexy, and despite the control she had over her features, her heart raced. He turned to walk away, but before he did, he looked her in the eyes so she could see the sincerity there when he delivered the final shock of the day. "And I really hope what you said isn't true because I *definitely* want something to do with you."

I hope you enjoyed Natalie and Aiden's sweet story of finding love! But we're not quite finished with them yet. Find out what happened when Aiden organizes a surprise for Nat that didn't quite go as planned. Click here for an exclusive bonus scene.

And coming next...Nick Newton has his hands full with his new daughter, but when his custody situation starts to get complicated, Charlotte Davis might be the only one who can help, if they can keep their feelings out of it.
Find out what happens with these two in Seeking Happily Ever After! And read an excerpt right after this!

Seeking Happily Ever After

Enjoy this excerpt of Seeking Happily Ever After

THE CRY JOLTED Nick Newton awake from a dead sleep. He grappled around in the dark for his glasses, followed by his cell phone.

It was quarter past two.

Too early. *Way* too early.

He held his breath, hoping whatever had caused her cry was a one-off. A fluke. Maybe he'd dreamed it and—

Another ear-shattering scream, this one more insistent than the last, split the air.

No, he definitely hadn't imagined it.

With a shake of his head, he threw the quilt aside and crossed the room to the crib he'd set up in the corner. "Hey there, princess." He reached down, but stopped short to see Amelia, seven months old, standing in the crib, her chubby fists clamped around the rails of the wooden crib. "This is new."

He smiled, marveling for a moment, even in his sleepy state, that she'd reached another milestone. It was the first time she'd pulled herself up in the crib. But the baby was in no mood for pleasantries. She cried out again, so Nick quickly gathered her up in his arms.

"What's this all about, kiddo?" He rocked her close. "Why are you awake? It's not a normal time of day. Daddy doesn't function at two a.m." If he hadn't been so exhausted, Nick would have laughed at himself. It wasn't that long ago that he was only getting the party started at two in the morning. Now, his party consisted of him, in a one-bedroom guest house, with a baby.

Things had changed.

Amelia had settled and was reaching up to his face with her chubby hands. He couldn't help but smile and bend down, offering his nose to be grabbed.

Yes, things certainly had changed. Absolutely everything had changed—for the better.

He yawned as Amelia's fingers clamped around his nose and squeezed.

Okay, maybe not everything had changed for the better. The lack of sleep he was still dealing with was definitely not an improvement.

At least before, when he was in the club partying, or entertaining a young lady or two in his fancy, overpriced penthouse until the sun came up, he could sleep well through the afternoon if he needed. And that was a very different type of exhaustion. Being the sole caregiver for a baby was next-level exhaustion. A bone-deep tired that never seemed to go away, no matter how much sleep he managed to get. Which, truthfully, was not much at all.

Just when he thought he had Amelia's schedule sorted out, she mixed it up on him.

"What do you need, princess? It's too early for breakfast, and…" He patted her bottom. The diaper was dry. He was too tired to think clearly, but if it wasn't the diaper, or hunger, then…what?

Nick shifted her in his arms and collapsed onto the couch in the guest house he was temporarily calling home. Amelia giggled. It was something she was doing more and more of lately, and he never tired of the noise. It was the sweetest thing he'd ever heard. To say that he was completely head over heels with the little girl would be a massive understatement. Never had another female had such an immense impact on him. Ever.

And that was saying something, considering for the last few years, since he and his best friend Damon Banks had sold their microchip design and had in turn become billionaires, Nick had turned into somewhat of a ladies' man. Which was a nice way of saying that, basically, he'd been sowing some wild oats and probably having too much fun. He'd had plenty of chances to meet *the one*.

Instead, he'd met the one who would make him a father.

Father.

The word still felt strange, even to think. Let alone to say aloud. Especially because despite his feelings for Amelia, and they were strong, he knew he wasn't her father. Not her biological one anyway. And that was going to be a problem. A big one.

If anyone found out.

It was something that occupied more and more of his thoughts over the last few weeks. Nick wasn't stupid; far from it. He rocked the baby, who'd finally lost interest in Nick's nose and was settling back into slumber, now content in his arms, and with his free hand, Nick pulled out his phone and clicked onto the file he'd received a few weeks earlier.

Jessica Silva.

It was all in there. Everything about Amelia's mother, the woman he'd dated—if you could even call a few hook-ups *dating*—over a year ago. Well over a year ago. Nick hadn't made his fortune being unsure about anything. He'd done the math. It didn't add up.

Amelia couldn't be his. Not biologically. He hadn't known that when Jessica's sister, Lacy, had appeared at his friend's wedding six months ago and unceremoniously dumped the baby with him, declaring him the father. It hadn't been until the days and weeks after when he knew it with certainty and had begun the investigation into where exactly Jessica was and why she didn't want to be a mother.

He scrolled through the file his private investigator had provided him with, even though he already knew it by heart.

There was nothing positive in it. Drugs. Alcohol. A series of men. Crappy apartments.

Until very recently.

Jessica had a steady job now. She was clean. She'd rented a townhouse with a small yard, in a decent neighborhood.

All good signs that she was getting her life together.

Nick clicked the phone off and gazed down at the now sleeping baby. His heart swelled with a love he didn't even know was possible to feel until Amelia had been dropped into his life.

And now, he couldn't imagine his life without her. Which was why he couldn't stop thinking about how to make sure he never would have to.

Charlotte Davis clicked through the photos her mother, Darlene, had emailed her for the real estate listing they were working on. Dishes piled on the counter, with every type of appliance ever invented covering every inch of space. Dirty dishtowels hung from the oven and refrigerator door.

Terrible.

Char tried not to roll her eyes and even though her mother hadn't asked, she jotted down a few notes about how to make the space look more appealing. It wouldn't take much to transform the space. She couldn't completely tell from the photos, but it looked like the kitchen itself was pretty nice, with a classic white tile backsplash and granite countertops that should be showcased instead of cluttered up.

Her parents, Darlene and Dwayne Davis, had been Glacier Falls' top real estate agents, and had recently come back out of retirement to take advantage of the market that was starting to heat up. In their absence, things had changed. A lot.

Not only was Glacier Falls starting to become a hot spot for city folk who were desperate to escape the hustle and bustle and experience the beauty of the mountains and all that was offered with small-town living, but there was more competition between agents. Maybe Char didn't have much experience in real estate, but it didn't take an expert to see that the photos her mother had sent over were terrible, and were not going to help get top dollar for the house.

Charlotte sighed and dropped her chin to her chest in a quick neck stretch.

She was grateful her parents had offered her the job, to be sure. But working for her parents when she was thirty-two years old because she'd just had to move home to live with them after an epically failed relationship was not exactly where Charlotte thought she would be in her life at this point.

Not even close.

But it was better than the alternative. She still shuddered when she thought about the poor decision-making that had led her to a relationship with Billy Grant, the man she'd met with an online dating app. He'd seemed like a good guy, if not a little rough around the edges, when they'd first started talking online and then moved things to phone and video calls. He'd really cared about her and what she was interested in and what she was doing. He proclaimed his love early and often. All signs that, in hindsight, should have alerted her, but her judgment was off.

No. It was completely malfunctioning.

It made her so angry with herself to think about how she'd fallen for him and had ignored all the red flags that had been so apparent. She was smarter than that. Yet, when he'd asked her to move across the country to be with him, she hadn't even hesitated. She quit her interior design job with an up-and-coming home builder in the city, sold everything she owned, pushed away her family's concerns and had jumped on a plane to Halifax. Only three months later, it had become clear that Billy Grant was not the sweet, caring, happily ever after she'd dreamed he was.

He was a controlling narcissist who'd managed to, piece by piece, strip away her self-esteem and self-worth until she didn't even recognize herself. It wasn't until after Christmas when her parents came for a visit that she had begun to see for herself that the situation she was in wasn't healthy. Still, it had taken a few more weeks for Charlotte to get up the courage to call her brother Jeremy for help.

And now she was home.

She stretched her arms over her head and, opting to talk to her mom in person about the terrible photos, pushed up from the kitchen table that she was using for a temporary office. Her parents had recently moved into an office space just off Main Street, but working from home gave her a little bit of space from them, or at the very least, the illusion of space. She loved her parents, she really did, but it was not normal to be living at home at her age.

She really needed to find a little apartment or something and move out. Of course, to do that, she'd need more money.

Charlotte tried not to think about the circle she was caught up in and instead pulled a sweater over her head. Maybe a morning walk would help to clear her head on more than one level.

April in Glacier Falls was unpredictable. The town was positioned in the valley so that, despite being tucked in among some of the most beautiful mountain ranges in the world, warm winds blew in early to provide an earlier-than-expected spring season. But that didn't mean that they couldn't be treated to a freak snowstorm at any time.

The sun was shining and warm on her face as Charlotte took her time walking to the office. She stopped to investigate some of the community garden beds for signs of life and found tulips and daffodils pushing up through the soil. It wouldn't be long before everything was in bloom and the grass was green again. Spring was Charlotte's favorite time in Glacier Falls. It had been too long since she'd spent the season in her hometown.

Maybe there were some positives with having to return home?

The smell of freshly baked honey buns floated on the breeze and Charlotte straightened.

Yes. There were definitely positives to being back in Glacier Falls.

The bells over the bakery door jingled as she stepped inside. She shut her eyes and inhaled deeply. Nothing smelled as good as delectable aromas coming from the ovens in the back of Sweetie Pies.

"Oh, sorry."

Charlotte jostled and almost fell over as the door to the bakery opened directly into her back. She probably should have gotten out of the way. "No," she said as she turned around to apologize. "It's my fault. I—Nick!"

Nick Newton was Glacier Fall's newest resident, who also

happened to be extremely handsome and ridiculously wealthy and therefore was the most sought-after bachelor in town. Never mind the fact that he had the sweetest little baby girl and pulled off the single dad thing adorably—not that Charlotte was in the market for a new boyfriend, because she absolutely was not. But she liked Nick. He was kind and sweet and a little bit dorky. And his baby, Amelia, was just about the most gorgeous child she'd ever seen. Charlotte couldn't help it; she had a soft spot for babies.

"Charlotte." Nick's face transformed into a smile. He always looked a little tired, but was it Char's imagination, or did he look stressed out, too? "I'm so sorry," he continued. "I didn't mean to crash into you. Are you okay?"

She rubbed her arm in reflex. "I'm fine. Totally my fault. I just walked in and the honey buns smelled so good, I couldn't take another step forward."

He laughed. "It *does* smell good in here. And that's exactly why we're here. A honey bun and some much needed coffee. Will you join us?"

It wasn't the only reason Nick was in the bakery that morning. Although, more often than not, Sweetie Pies was becoming his go-to breakfast place. He really was going to have to develop a few skills in the kitchen and soon, or he was going to gain twenty pounds and Amelia's first word would be sugar, for all the time he spent at the bakery.

But that morning, it was more than just the lure of sugar and caffeine that had brought him to the bakery. Nick needed to think. And oddly enough, he'd always done his best thinking when he was surrounded by people in a busy place. His friend and old business partner, Damon, had needed silence to do his work, insisting that a quiet space allowed his mind to take over and the ideas to come to him. But Nick was the opposite. The quiet made it impossible to silence his own thoughts long enough to get the answers he needed.

And he needed answers.

After Amelia's early morning wake-up, he'd been unable to get back to sleep and had instead decided to do a little more research into his situation before calling his lawyer at the much more reasonable hour of five a.m. Nick knew Chris was awake, and no doubt already at his desk. He was the only person who worked harder than Nick and Damon—when they'd been working on their design—which was why Chris Montgomery had been the perfect choice for their team.

He hadn't been surprised to hear from Nick, either. "Have you thought more about your situation?" Chris never was one for small talk.

"It's all I can think about."

Chris was one of the very few people who knew the truth about baby Amelia's parentage. At least as much as anyone knew. Only Jessica knew who her father actually was. At least, Nick assumed she knew. But that could turn out to be a pretty big assumption, given Jessica's lifestyle at the time.

"And?" Chris had presented Nick with a few options for how to proceed with Amelia. There was only one really good choice, but that didn't stop Nick from feeling badly about it. "Nick, you know there's only one thing to do."

He did know.

"If you want that little girl to stay with you, it's the only choice."

Nick swallowed. "I know."

"So you want me to proceed with adoption?"

He nodded. "Yes."

Adoption would mean that Amelia was his and no one could take her from him. He had the best legal team money could buy, and Chris had assured him that they'd do everything they could to make it come together quickly and as painlessly as possible. Which no doubt also meant it would cost him. But Nick didn't care. He only cared about making sure Amelia's future was secure and safe.

He'd grown up without a father. And a mother who might as well have not been there most of the time, she was so lost in addiction. To both men and alcohol. It wasn't fair to compare Jessica with his mother, not when he didn't know. Not really. But it also wasn't fair to Amelia to roll those dice. She deserved more than the start he got in life, and he would go to the ends of the earth to give it to her.

Chris had spent the next fifteen minutes reminding him that it wouldn't be easy, and they'd have to contact the birth mother, get her to sign over parental rights or have her proved unfit, neither of which was what Nick wanted to hear. And he'd told him as much. If Jessica didn't agree, it could get messy and Amelia didn't deserve that. He also knew, thanks to Chris, that it wasn't easy for a single father to proceed with adoption, particularly when he wasn't actually the biological father.

Still. There weren't any other options.

Nick had agreed to send over the information from the private investigator regarding Jessica's whereabouts and put the wheels in motion.

But that was a few hours ago, and he still hadn't sent it. Because he knew exactly what would happen if he did.

Everything would change, and the peaceful, little, quiet life he'd been trying to build in Glacier Falls would become anything but.

At least for the time being, he could enjoy the quiet…and Charlotte. Nick snuck a glance back toward the table where he'd left her and Amelia to get settled while he went to grab coffee and snacks.

He smiled the way he always seemed to when he saw Charlotte Davis. From the first time he'd met her, something drew him to her. Sure, he knew she was coming out of a terrible relationship and was not in any way ready to date again, but he wasn't either. It was a detail that almost made him like her more. She was sweet and funny and absolutely stunning. Something about her—a quiet, thoughtful undercurrent—let Nick know there was a lot more to her than she showed people on the surface. In a different situation, he would have already asked her out.

Charlotte wasn't like any of the women he'd met before. Which wasn't too hard a feat, really, considering when he and Damon were busy at work on their microchip design, there hadn't been any time for women, and definitely no time for dating. When he was invested in a project, he went all in, with complete focus.

When they'd finally finished and sold the microchip design for more money than either Nick or Damon could properly understand, Nick had gone completely off the rails and, true to form, became one hundred percent invested in the party lifestyle. Women and partying. Traveling the globe. Drinking too much everywhere he went and largely living a life that had started to scare him on more than one occasion. He'd woken up more than once unsure of where he was, who he was with, or how he'd gotten there.

He might still be that way, too, if Amelia hadn't come into his life. Because the moment the baby girl was dropped in his lap, once again his focus shifted—one hundred percent. Only now he was completely devoted to a tiny baby girl.

And that's where his focus would stay, at least until she was legally his and safe from the type of childhood he'd grown up with. Maybe then...he'd be able to expand his attentions and think about finding someone to share his life with. His gaze lingered on Charlotte, who'd pulled Amelia from her stroller and bounced her on her lap, making the baby giggle. He smiled, a warmth in his chest beginning to grow. *Maybe even—*

"Hey, handsome."

He spun around to see Georgia behind the counter, her trademarked bright smile on her face.

"What can I get you? Something sweet, I hope?" She lowered her eyelids and wiggled her eyebrows.

"Sorry." Nick shook his head. "I was daydreaming for a minute."

"About me, I hope?"

"Always." He couldn't help but return the innocent flirting. "And those sweet buns of yours." Georgia was one of those women who made it easy to flirt with them. She was bubbly and fun, and every morning when he dragged his exhausted self into her bakery, she was there with a smile and a coffee. Two of his favorite things.

They exchanged a few more minutes of banter while Nick placed his standard order, adding an extra coffee and bun for Charlotte, an addition that earned him an extra eyebrow raise and a glance in Charlotte's direction. There was a question in Georgia's eye, but Nick didn't rise to the bait.

If he was ever ready to date again, Georgia should be an obvious candidate. She was easygoing, fun, flirty, and cute. She owned her own business and as far as Nick knew, she had her life together and was in a good place. On paper, she seemed like a perfect choice for dating. But something was missing. Something he couldn't quite pinpoint.

He accepted his order and paid, leaving a generous tip the way he always did. When she gave him a wink as a thank-you, he returned it with one of his own before taking the tray and turning around.

The moment Nick saw Charlotte and Amelia together, a giant smile crossed his face again and once more the warmth in his gut bloomed. Seeing her with Amelia stirred up all kinds of really good feelings he didn't have any real experience with, and more importantly, whatever was missing when he looked at Georgia fell perfectly into place when he looked at Charlotte.

Read the rest of Charlotte and Nick's story right after this in Seeking Happily Ever After.

About the Author

Elena Aitken is a USA Today Bestselling Author of more than forty romance and women's fiction novels. The mother of 'grown up' twins, Elena now lives with her very own mountain man in the heart of the very mountains she writes about. She can often be found with her toes in the lake and a glass of wine in her hand, dreaming up her next book and working on her own happily ever after.

To learn more about Elena:
www.elenaaitken.com
elena@elenaaitken.com